5 DEAD WOMEN

5 DEAD WOMEN

Order this book online at www.trafford.com
or email orders@trafford.com

Most Trafford titles are also available at major online book retailers.

Author photograph by Brian Durham
Original book cover artwork and design by Diane Cope

Printed in the United States of America.

ISBN: 978-1-4269-5550-1 (sc)
ISBN: 978-1-4269-5551-8 (hc)
ISBN: 978-1-4269-5552-5 (e)

Library of Congress Control Number: 2011900671

Trafford rev. 01/14/2011

www.trafford.com

North America & international
toll-free: 1 888 232 4444 (USA & Canada)
phone: 250 383 6864 • fax: 812 355 4082

ACKNOWLEDGEMENTS

The more I live the more I am blessed, and the more I definitely learn. I have always believed that God places individuals in our lives for a reason. These are the people who have shown me nothing but love and support, and who have always put a smile on my face even when there was nothing to smile about:

Ellen Prescod-Forde - No words needed there, you have been and will continue to be my sister and my best friend and I love you, love you, love you.

Tracy Forde - You are my voice of reason and I know that you *always* have my back. You will forever be my "duck" and I will always be your "frog" even if no one understands what the heck we are talking about.

My children, Kennedi and C.J. - You continue to inspire me everyday with your strength, understanding, patience and intelligence that is way beyond your years. I want you to know that I take my job and responsibility as your mother very seriously and I love you unconditionally and will always be there for you no matter the circumstances.

Lisa Legall-Belgrave - You came into my life when we were both 11 year old little girls. We lost touch, but thank God for bringing us into each other's lives once again. You are a very inspiring and uplifting friend. Thanks for everything Lisa; let's not lose touch with each other ever again.

Diane Cope - Looking at the two of us, no one would think that we have so much in common and that we have so much fun together. It just goes to show that friendship comes from the heart; deep within the heart. When all I saw was darkness, you reminded me why I set out on this journey in the first place; and in your gentle, loving way, you pushed me to continue on to that light at the end of the tunnel. I never get tired of our late night telephone calls with lots of giggles.

Liesel Daisley - Our paths crossed due to similar circumstances in our lives which were not so pleasant. Somehow, we have both used those past adversities to propel us forward. When women bond together for the betterment of themselves and a genuine passion to help others, I feel like they can move mountains. We are both survivors with a purpose and a reason!!! Thanks so very much for your support from so far away.

Kathy Knight - What can I say to you to make you understand and see just how much your love and constant support means to me? There is such unconditional love and genuine concern and friendship between us. I love the fact that we can talk for hours about nothing, but yet about everything and I can truly confide in you and you in me as cousins first, friends second. You are such a beautiful person Kathy!

DEDICATION

This book is dedicated to all the hardworking women out there who are facing any type of adversity; God hasn't forgotten about you. Remember, whatever you go through in this life, ALWAYS choose to be a SURVIVOR!!!

To my precious Kennedi and CJ; Mommy loves you very, very much.

To my mother, Nolan Hope-Butler; the value of a mother's love is immeasurable.

To Thelma Hope and NewDaisie Lashley, may you rest in peace; your love still surrounds and guides me everyday.

PREFACE

"Where am I?" Alex couldn't remember how she got to the beach; she didn't even live anyway where near a beach. *How the hell did I get here and where is here?*

As Alex looked around she realized that she was not alone, nor was she the only one looking surprised and shocked. Three other women were all sitting on the sand just gazing around, with their mouths wide open. Alex tried her best to remember exactly what had happened or what was happening; then she realized that she must be dreaming.

She walked over to the three women and introduced herself; "Hi, I am Alexis Jones". The other women all smiled and one by one said their names; Megan nervously extended her hand and gave a weak smile. She was a tiny, timid woman, and Alex had to ask her to repeat her name. Alex couldn't help but think that Megan's fiery red hair definitely did not match her personality.

Brea was next, she got up and dusted the sand of her clothes and gave an exuberant smile. "My name is Brea, Brea Ottinger,

I am from......" Alex wasn't listening to what Brea was saying she was staring at the other woman sitting with her legs pulled up to her chin, rocking back and forth and crying. Alex walked away from Brea, who was still talking, and walked toward the crying woman. As Alex bent down and placed her hand on the woman's shoulder, the woman immediately pulled away still screaming hysterically.

Now the rest of the women all turned to Alex and the screaming lady, who kept repeating over and over, "No, no, no, no, no". Megan stood back, way back, she was looking around and pinching her arm; she looked up into the sky, and she looked out onto the water. She nervously looked at another figure slowly walking towards them. Megan looked at the rest of the women and said to them, her voice cracking, "Do any of you know where we are and how we got here?" She then added, "I pinched myself and I cannot feel anything, it is eerily quiet and there is no one or anything else in sight, just us. Please tell me where we are?"

It was then that Alex realized that all the panic was justified; she couldn't for the life of her figure out where she was. She looked up just as the other woman that was walking towards them finally approached the small group. The new visitor looked at Alex and slowly said, "I think I know where we are, oh my God we are........"

PART 1 – MEET SHELDON

Life Is Good

Sheldon awoke to a tiny wet nose nuzzling hers; it was little Kayla. Sheldon smiled as she hugged her two year old daughter and then planted her head with a million kisses. Sheldon couldn't help but gulp back a tear at how lucky she was. Married 12 years to the man of her dreams Chris, who back in college had literally swept her off her feet, her life was the closest thing to perfect that she could have ever imagined. Sheldon swung her feet off of the bed, still carrying Kayla in her arms, and headed towards the bathroom.

She set Kayla down on the bathroom counter and glanced at herself in the mirror, "not bad for being pregnant three times" she quipped to herself. She was right, for she still had that beautiful tight, taut body that she had when she was 18 and her breasts were so perky, you would have never guessed that she breastfed one child, let alone three. Sheldon admitted to herself that she was a bit vain, but very humble.

"Who am I kidding, there is not a humble bone in this perfect body that God blessed me with" she chuckled to herself.

As Sheldon got ready to start her day, she couldn't help but think back to her chance meeting with Chris. She never in a million years thought that Chris would even look in her direction. She was by all description a "ghetto girl", right down the three pairs of bamboo earrings and heavy black lip liner. None of the girls had liked her, mainly because they were afraid of her.

She had grown up in a very rough neighborhood, and endured hardships that no child should ever have to endure. She watched her mother have baby after baby, almost every other year with different men; men who came and left like her front door was a turnstile at a train station.

Sheldon couldn't understand why her mother didn't see a pattern and stop, at least by baby number three.

Sheldon was determined to get the hell out of there; one way or another; she could never see her life like her mom's. So she used her brains, and while the other girls in the neighborhood were hanging on the corner and having babies starting as early as in middle school, Sheldon chose another direction. She stayed in her room and studied as much as she could.

Sure her sisters and friends, even her mother laughed at her and even mocked her for her choices, but Sheldon didn't care. She saw a light far, far ahead that they couldn't see; and once she got that full scholarship to college, she never looked back.

CHAPTER 2

The Tough Chick

She tried her best to mingle and fit in with the other girls at college, but no one gave her a chance. She dressed differently, she spoke differently and try as she might she just could not make any friends.

Sheldon, now looking into the mirror at her reflection she thought to herself, "who is ghetto now, who has all the friends now?"

Chris was paired up with Sheldon for a class project and at first he was quite intimidated by this beautiful caramel skinned woman. His friends laughed and joked to him to hide his wallet and his jewelry. But Chris being the gentleman that he was did his best to treat this, even though very different, young woman with the utmost respect. He was careful not to make her mad though.

After a couple weeks of hanging out and working on their project, their conversations turned to family life and soon they found themselves being the best of friends and confiding in each other. Chris realized that Sheldon was really a misunderstood soul.

Yes, she had this tough exterior and dressed and acted differently, but he decided that she had only conformed to her surroundings.

Chris started to develop feelings for this "ghetto girl". He pushed them to the back of his mind, it was impossible. His parents would have a coronary, they would disown him, they might even put a hit out on him.

Chris' parents, coming from a long line of judges, lawyers, doctors, senators, they already had the perfect girl picked out for him; a five foot nine blond hair, green eyed princess whose family had more money than God.

All the while Sheldon was dreaming about how wonderful her life would be if she was to marry someone like Chris. She would NEVER be able to take him home to meet her family, instead she would tell him that she was adopted and furthermore, her adoptive parents had died.

Yes, she would have it good, she would not end up like her welfare getting, weave wearing, food stamp getting, whore of a mother and her sisters, who all but the youngest one had at least three children already; with no daddy or daddies anywhere to be found.

Sheldon had started to feel the sparks between her and Chris, but she was careful. She was aware that guys like him only screwed around with girls like her in the dark, but then they marry their white queens. Sheldon was smarter than that though, she knew what she wanted in life, she knew where she came from and 'so help her God she wasn't going back'.

She was going to be everything to him; he would not be able to resist her. First of all she had to change her appearance. Luckily she had a decent paying part time job at a department store and even though the money wasn't what she would have liked it to be, she got a great discount and got first dibs at the marked down merchandise. After studying the other sales girls, she started asking them for some fashion tips.

CHAPTER 3

You Never Know What's Coming

On any given day, Sheldon would show up to class wearing jeans so damn tight that you could see the imprint of her tampon string. They also hung so low on her ass that it looked like she had two separate asses; one bare and the other covered. Her acrylic nails were a good two inches long, and her nail polish was always representative of the holiday or season or just the mood that she was in.

There was a ring on every finger, cheap ten karat gold rings that she had either acquired from a pawn shop back home or borrowed from one of her sisters and never returned.

Sheldon always thought that Payless Shoe Store was the shit. She could never figure out how shoes that looked so good could be so cheap.

Even though Sheldon had beautiful brown hair, curly hair; the kind of hair that made her sisters jealous, she still chose to cover it up with cheap wigs.

Sheldon's mother couldn't pinpoint who her father was; she did know that he must have either been "one o' dem half white men, or one o' dem white men" as she would always tell Sheldon. Either way, Sheldon had long, curly, thick hair; the kind of hair that most girls back in her neighborhood paid $24.99 a bunch to have. It didn't say much for her fashion sense either, that her god awful wigs always matched her nails.

Chris was at first a bit embarrassed to be seen with this person who was the polar opposite of him. Chris wore Doc Martens or Ralph Lauren shoes, and had probably never even heard of Payless Shoes; he was almost always in a Ralph Lauren buttoned down shirt. The only jewelry he wore was a two toned Rolex watch that his grandfather, God rest his soul, had given him for his high school graduation.

One evening after studying for a test, Chris worked up the courage to ask Sheldon a question that he had been aching to ask her for a very long time; why did she choose to dress like that. He half expected her to slap the shit out of him, but instead Sheldon broke down crying.

This tough looking, ghetto chick poured her heart out to him; she told him of her family life, and she told the truth, not the lies she had planned, she told him that she would love to dress like the other girls at school, but this was the only way that she knew.

CHAPTER 4

I Think I am Falling

Chris suddenly realized that over the course of a couple of the months, all the time he had spent with Sheldon, that he had subconsciously fallen unconditionally and undeniably in love with her. But he knew that she probably saw him as this rich snob who looked down on her; when in fact what he saw was a beautiful, intelligent, sexy, driven, outspoken girl, who by no fault of hers, had been born into less than favorable circumstances.

She was not her mother, she couldn't help where she came from; she had worked hard in school, received a full scholarship and was now top in her class.

Nothing was ever given to her; he admired that. Plus he had fun with her, not like these uppity girls his parents always fixed him up with. Sheldon was a blast to be around, after a while, Chris forgot what she was wearing, how she talked or how people looked at them; the seemingly odd, very odd couple.

Things naturally progressed between the two, a friendship turned into a blossoming romance. He could not stay away from her; they held hands and kissed in public, much to the dismay of Chris' Polo playing college buddies. All the while, Sheldon still couldn't comprehend what had happened.

She didn't have to lie or even twist the truth, and yet this rich, handsome, eligible guy had fallen for her, *for her*, wow! For the first time in her life Sheldon understood what unconditional love and friendship really was.

Even though they were close, very close, their friendship and love was not that of the seemingly average college couple. Chris and Sheldon did not immediately jump into bed. They both had their own reasons; Chris being the gentleman that he was did not want to seem pushy like a horny little school boy. And Sheldon, she wanted something more than just sex, plus in the back of her mind she was still thinking that maybe Chris just wanted to get some 'different booty' and then move on to a suitable woman from his own station in life.

The friendship and closeness that they shared was thrilling enough to sustain their relationship, but they both knew that they could not hold out much longer.

Nearing the end of their third year in college, Chris called Sheldon and gave her an invitation that really surprised her. He told her that he was going to the family's summer home in the Hamptons in New York for a week to clear his head and plan his future, and that he wanted nothing more than for her to accompany him.

Sheldon was both excited and taken aback by the invite, but timidly and with much embarrassment told him that even though she would love to go, that she didn't have any money for a plane ticket. At hearing this, Chris laughed and reassured her that since he invited her that he would be taking care of all of her expenses. When she finally said yes, Chris admitted that he had already purchased her plane ticket, so the only answer that he was prepared to hear was yes. She smiled.

Sheldon had heard about the Hamptons before, but never in a million years had she ever imagined that she would ever be going there. Wow, if only her friends from back home could see her now.

When the plane landed at La Guardia airport, Sheldon thought that she was at their final destination, so imagined her surprise when Chris rented a car and informed her that they had about an eighty five mile drive to East Hampton. He said that they could have changed planes and flown into MacArthur Airport which was only fifty miles away, but he wanted them to have a good old fashion road trip, so that she could see the sights.

Chris was very affectionate with Sheldon. She had thought that maybe he would keep his distance from her, seeing that they were out and away from the college campus, and amongst his kind no less, but to her surprise his hand was either across her shoulder, caressing the small of her back, or he was just plain holding her hand.

Sheldon was starting to feel safe and secure with Chris, but she still had somewhat of a guard up for fear of getting hurt and ending up looking like a fool.

CHAPTER 5

What A Beautiful Sunset

When they pulled into his parents' summer home, Sheldon could not hide the look of utter astonishment on her face. She knew that they were rich, but if this was just a summer home, then she knew that they had to be loaded.

Not only was it almost as big as the apartment complex that she grew up in, but it was right on the beach. As they exited the car, Sheldon thought that she had died and gone to heaven. She thought that places like these only existed on television and in the movies. If she had thought the outside of the home was impressive she was not in store for what met her on the inside.

Chris described the house to her as if he was a real estate agent trying to make a sale. The 1835 vintage traditional Hamptons home had six bedrooms, five baths, formal dining room, chef's kitchen, a fireplace and an ocean view from almost every room. Sheldon couldn't help but think that the house evoked some type of authentic charm of what she imagined would have been that era. It was just a stone's throw away from the water's edge.

Chris had asked her to get her stuff unpacked so that they could go into town for some supplies. Sheldon was in a dream, one that she preferred to never, ever awake from.

That evening after dinner, which consisted of a frozen pasta meal and a bottle of Sangiovese that Chris had gotten from his parents' wine pantry, Chris suggested that they go for a walk along the beach. When Chris had to explain the wine choice to her, she listened and learned.

The only wine that she had been familiar with was wine coolers, 'is a wine cooler actually wine?' Either way, she was very impressed as Chris not only explained to her the wine he chose for dinner, but he took her to the wine pantry and gave her a crash course in wine 101.

CHAPTER 6

An Unforgettable Moment

Sheldon just knew that she was going to wake up from her dream at any moment; here she was a black girl from one of the toughest neighborhoods in Tennessee, who had never been exposed to anything even remotely close to this type of lifestyle before and here she was staying in a multimillion dollar home in the Hamptons.

As they strolled along the beach, Chris put his arm around her waist and leaned down and kissed her neck. She looked out onto the ocean and thought to herself that she would never experience another moment like this in her life. It was perfect, a kiss on the neck, while standing on the beach at sunset with a man who seemed to obviously adore her.

It was at that precise moment, at sunset, that Sheldon knew that she had truly fallen in love with Christain Kingsland.

Sheldon realized that they had that stretch of private beach all to themselves. Chris had brought a blanket along and they spread it down on the sand and just held each other as they watched the curved top of the sun disappear behind the horizon as if saying goodbye to them and only the two of them.

Chris had held her hand and looked into her eyes and without saying a word had given her the best kiss of her life. It was soft, very soft, lingering and passionate; but most of all she felt love and desire, like he was kissing her with everything that he had. Sheldon felt things that she had never felt before; what she had felt was pure, sincere, and extremely overwhelming.

As Chris gently laid her down on the blanket, he looked directly into her eyes, and told her how much he loved her and wanted to be with her every waking moment. By this time Sheldon was in tears, tears of joy and tears of relief, for she had waited for this moment for a very long time.

She reached over and gently pulled his vintage tee over his head and kissed his chest with the gentleness of a fairy testing her gossamer wings for the very first time. She continued on up towards his neck until she found his lips once again.

Chris had taken her face in his hands and after staring into her eyes for what seemed like an eternity, had kissed her like never before.

Right there on that beach, Chris had undressed her and had literally kissed every inch of her body, until tears were streaming down her face and onto the blanket. When he cupped her breast, he had quietly moaned that she had the perfect body. Sheldon closed her eyes and found herself on such a high that she knew she had to have this man to herself for ever and ever.

As they both continued to explore the unchartered territory that was each other, it seemed like they could not get enough of one another. Chris had whispered to her and asked her if she was sure that she was ready, and she remembered thinking to herself,

Ready? I am so ready right now that if he kisses me again I am going to explode..

He had then slid on top of her and for what seemed like another eternity had continued to kiss and caress her. All the while Sheldon was nervous, but she was ready; especially when she felt him pressing against her belly.

Chris had made his way in between her legs and had started to enter her when he was met with the tightness and resistance that could only have meant one thing. He looked down into Sheldon's eyes and with the ease, caution, precision and finesse of landing a 747 jumbo jet on a slick runway, he entered her. He had felt a slight tearing, but Sheldon didn't seem to be in any discomfort. It was then that he had leaned down and whispered in her ear,

"Why didn't you tell me sweetheart? This makes me love you all the more".

"It was not something I wanted to shout from the roof tops" she had quietly responded.

"Am I hurting you Sheldon? Please let me know of I am hurting you."

"No" she had moaned, "no, you are not hurting me sweetheart."

The love and passion was so intense between them that Chris was only able to hold out for what had seemed like a very brief moment. And as they both reached that pinnacle of no return, Sheldon had wrapped her legs tightly around Chris' back as they looked into each other's eyes. They had erupted with such force and passion that they both sobbed.

CHAPTER 7

Just Shout It From The Roof Top

Chris lost a lot of his friends once they realized that he and Sheldon were more than friends. He was hoping that word would not get back to his parents before he had a chance to break the news to them.

When Chris took her to dinner to finally meet his parents they were so appalled that they threatened that if she stayed, that they would not be eating dinner, because they refused to eat with her. His parents had vowed to disown him if he didn't stop seeing this 'gutter trash'.

Sheldon just knew that Chris would ask her to leave in favor of his parents because he did not want to lose his inheritance or his good family name. But to her surprise, Chris flatly told his parents that they could take all their money and dump it in the ocean for all he cared, because no amount of money in the world could replace Sheldon.

He told them that he loved her and that they better get used to it because she was going to be his wife. Sheldon almost fainted, "Chris wants to marry me?" she couldn't hold back the tears.

CHAPTER 8

Yeah, I look Good

As Sheldon continued to stare at her now 32 year old body in her bathroom mirror, she remembered that for that visit to his parents' house, she had went out of her way to look 'normal'. She had discarded that godforsaken red wig, and washed, conditioned and flat ironed her hair. She couldn't help but wonder why she had never done that to her hair before, it was simply gorgeous.

Sheldon then had the acrylic removed from her nails, and had her own nails neatly manicured with clear nail polish. She visited the Chanel makeup counter and got a crash course in applying makeup the right way. She even got her eyebrows neatly waxed and arched.

Next she found the cutest top that could have doubled as a dress for a night out on the town, and she paired it with dark washed skinny jeans. She had switched her usual 'bamboo, around the way girl' earrings for an adorable pair of gold chandelier ones.

For the first time ever, Sheldon went to the shoe department at the store she worked at. She couldn't believe the price of these shoes, how could she afford them? She browsed the sale rack and came upon a pair of BCBG heels, they were black leather and strappy, she fell in love with them. They were a little more than she expected to spend, even on sale they were still $79.95. There goes her spending money for the next month she thought.

But to her surprise, when she got to the cash register they were not only an additional percentage off, but she had completely forgotten about her employee discount.

She ended up paying $30.00 for shoes that were originally $150.00. No guy had ever taken her home to meet his parents before, and she was determined to look her best.

When she saw her reflection in the mirror, she almost cried.

If only my mother and the people from my old neighborhood could see me now, she had said to herself, almost in tears.

When Chris saw her, even though he was blown away by how good she looked, somehow he wasn't too shocked, because this is the girl he always saw when he looked at her. Her outside now matched her inside. He knew in his heart that she would be his wife, no matter what.

Sheldon realized that she was still standing in front of the mirror admiring herself and reminiscing while little Kayla was smearing her favorite lipstick all over the mirror. As Sheldon came back to the present, she yelled to her son Ashton to please come get Kayla and put her in her high chair so that she could continue getting ready. She had to get the two older ones off to school.

CHAPTER 9

I Love This Woman

Sheldon took a hot shower and combed through her closet of now high end brand name clothes for an outfit for that day. She settled on a simple pair of khaki capris with a pale yellow sweater set and a pair of chocolate brown ballerina flats to finish off the outfit.

She decided to go with her now signature pearls which Chris had given to her as a first anniversary present. Her hair was done in long flowing curls and her makeup was lightly applied. Over the years she had mastered the art of makeup, and now had it down to a science; she was always flawless.

As she glanced on the floor next to her bed, she saw a note on the floor. She picked it up and realized that it was from Chris. *It must have fallen to the floor when Kayla jumped into our bed this morning*, Sheldon thought.

Dear Shel,

I awoke this morning and looked over and saw your beautiful face. I lifted my eyes to the heavens and thanked God for blessing me with such a wonderful wife and mother to our three precious children. I was so overwhelmed with emotion that I had to write you this note. Shel, you are everything I could ever dream of and more. I just wanted to remind you how much I love and appreciate you. Have a wonderful day, and as always I cannot wait to get home tonight to see your perfect, smiling face. Remember that evening in the Hamptons on that old blanket? Wink, wink.

I love you more than life,

Chris

(P.S Please don't forget your appointment at 11:00am with Dr. Braman; If you do not want to take Kayla with you, I have aunt Rosa on standby to babysit).

Sheldon smiled as she thought about her husband's thoughtfulness and how much he loved her. Also about how ironic it seemed that as she was reminiscing about that night in the Hamptons, so was he.

She did in fact remember her doctor's appointment, but had called a couple days before and postponed it. Sheldon figured that it was just a routine annual exam and besides, she had better things to do than go to the doctor again only to hear that she was just fine and , "see you next year, Mrs. Kingsland". She wanted to go shopping, to the cleaners and she had to meet her friend Patty for lunch and of course she was way overdue for a pedicure.

No, there was no time to waste on a doctor's appointment today. She felt great, sure she had lost a few pounds but she had cut down on her carb intake and was taking a pilates class a couple times a week, so that was expected. She looked fabulous, *the doctor can take a chill pill for now, plus think of the money that Chris will save on my no show doctor visit.*

Sheldon walked downstairs to find that their housekeeper of seven years, Mona had already cleared the breakfast dishes and had assisted the children in getting ready for school.

A load of laundry was already in the washing machine and Sheldon's Special K breakfast bar was on the kitchen counter next to a glass of freshly squeezed orange juice. Sheldon liked Mona, but she was careful not to get too personal with her, after all Mona came from the same neighborhood that she had come from.

Sheldon was adamant that Mona's relationship with the family remained strictly on an employer and employee one. She always felt that Chris was way too nice to the help.

Little did Sheldon know that *'the help'* was really not too fond of her either. Mona simply could not stand her; yes, Mona was happy that a girl from her side of town hit the jackpot by marrying into one of the richest families in the state, but she always felt that Sheldon had forgotten where she came from.

Sheldon had no idea that Mona was her mother's friend, and that Mona secretly took pictures of the three kids for her mother to see. Sheldon's mother Mildred had no access to her grandchildren at all. They went to a private school, and she would have bet anything that they didn't know that they had family members on their mother's side of the family.

So one day when Mildred's friend and neighbor was casually telling her about the family she was now working for, Sheldon's mother almost choked on her coffee. Mildred had realized that the rich family that her neighbor Mona was working for was in fact her own flesh and blood daughter Sheldon and her husband!

Mildred could not believe that her daughter was practically a millionaire and yet she was stuck in a housing development and still living off food stamps and the government.

She had long time ago accepted Sheldon's ungratefulness and her selfish ways. Mildred thought, *yes, I was not a very good mother, hell, I was a bad mother but I did the best I knew how; anybody would tell you, my children never went hungry and even though they did not have a lot of clothes but they were always clean and neat.*

I wish I had learnt my lesson before I ended up with six damn children, but they are here now and I cannot change that. I long ago asked God for forgiveness, and I accept all the mistakes that I made.

I cannot complain about my life now, I just have to do the best that I can and know that God has forgiven me; even if my daughter hasn't.

Mildred thought that her three grandchildren were the most beautiful creatures on earth, and she was so proud. They did not look like they had any black in them at all, they all looked 100% white.

But Sheldon's husband *was* white and Sheldon's father was also white, at least that is what Mildred thought he was. She wanted nothing more than to hold her grandchildren, and hug them and kiss them, and spend some time with them; as any grandmother would.

But the reality of it was, that Sheldon would never even allow them anywhere near that side of town. So until a miracle was handed down from God almighty himself, Mildred had to settle for seeing her three grandchildren in the pictures that Mona secretly brought to her.

Sheldon hollered for Molly and Ashton to hurry while she was securing Kayla into her car seat. One of the things that Sheldon loved about being a stay at home mom was that she got to take her kids to school and pick them up and be a full time mother.

As the other two kids got into Sheldon's new Calla White Audi Q7 with the Limestone Gray interior, she again could not believe how great a life she had. She already had a BMW X5 when Chris surprised her for her 32nd birthday with a brand new Audi.

He knew her tastes down to a science, and when that garage door had opened up and she saw the new Audi sitting there with the big red bow on the hood, all she could do was fall to her knees and sob.

CHAPTER 10

The Good Life

Sheldon dropped four year old Molly and ten year old Ashton off at their prestigious $20,000 a year private school and decided to go to the cleaners first since they were opened early. Then off to get her pedicure, but she remembered that she wore ballerina flats that were obviously not open toed.

So she then back tracked to a little boutique that she probably would not have even been allowed to go into a few years ago, and purchased a pair of Ralph Lauren high heeled shoes, with the toes out of course. She paid way too much for them, but when you have an American Express black card with no limit, who cares?

As she was walking out of the boutique her cell phone rang; it was Chris checking in to see if she was on her way to her doctor's appointment. She told Chris that she decided to postpone her doctor visit because she knew that she was fine.

Chris got a little annoyed and reminded her how important it was to keep her annual appointments for her checkup. Sheldon got a little annoyed as well and thought, *'it's my body'*, but said out loud to Chris that she didn't cancel it, she just postponed it and was going to call to reschedule. Chris reminded her that it was of the utmost importance to have these annual check ups.

"Come on honey, I wouldn't be hounding you if I didn't love you, I want us to grow old together" he added.

Sheldon smiled and assured him that she would call the doctor's office and reschedule.

CHAPTER 11

Something Doesn't Feel Right

Months went by and Sheldon forgot all about the promised doctor visit. But she couldn't hide the fact that something was not quite right with her body; for starters, she was constipated more than what might be considered to be normal. She took laxatives and they would work, but she always felt like there was more to come out and somehow things were a little "backed up".

So she ordered a colon cleansing kit from a late night infomercial, and waited for the results. Yes, she got some relief, but as soon as she got through with the colon cleansing regimen, she felt constipated again.

Sheldon remembered when a bowel moment was like getting a load off, "literally"; but now when she did manage to go, after straining and panting for what seem like forever , all she got was an almost pencil thin string of stool to show for it.

Even though she was getting increasingly concerned, she decided to keep it from Chris. While she was going through the colon cleansing program and Chris would snuggle up to her during the night and start to caress her, she nervously told him that she was on her period and was cramping and hurting. Chris being the ever caring and understanding husband never questioned or pressured her.

One afternoon in late Spring, Sheldon opened her mailbox to find a letter from a very familiar address. She started to rip it up and discard it without reading it, but curiosity got the better of her. With Kayla perched on her lap, she read;

Dear Sheldoniqua, ("Oh My God, she used my birth name" Sheldon exclaimed) *I hope that this leter finds you well. I attemted to write this letter to your many times over the years, but each time I wuld either stopped or I tore it up. This time I have the corage to finaly talk to you. First of all, Sheldoniqua, I am sorry, sorry for every single thing. I am sorry for the nights I left you to babysit the yunger childdrins while I was out parttying, or doing whatever I was doing. I am sorry for having so many men in and out of your life, I am sorry for bringing you into the world to live under such hurribble konditions. I am sorry that I was not a smart mohther, I am sorry that I did not come to your colege gradurartion; I wasn't invited, but I was going to come in the back and sit just to see you. I couldn't even aford a bust tiket to come. I am sorry for so many tings that I have stoped counting. Most of all I am sorry that I do not have a chance to see my grnchilren. Please, please forgive me, I askked god for forgiveness and I know he forrgive me. Now I just need to here it from you Sheldoniqua.*

I bearrly live on the litle foodstamps I get each month, and I do odd jobs hear and there cleening and stuff like that. I am not asking you for a handout but if I could clean your house a few days a week, or babysit mayybe you could pay me. I do not want any hand outs, I am wiling to work. Please Sheldoniqua, it took a lot for me to come to you like this. If I do not get anyting out of this, at least please let me see my granchilren. I would do anyting in the world to see you and my granchilren. If I never hear from you, I just want you to know how sorry I am for everything and how much I love you. I would give my life for you Sheldoniqua. I do not have a telefone, but if you write me with your number, I can find a way to call you. Please, please forgive me.

You one an only motther

Mildred

By now Sheldon was fuming mad, thinking about how the hell Mildred got her address, and on top of everything had the nerve to ask for a fucking job!!!

"And how did she know that I have kids; how did she know anything about me? It must be Mona" Sheldon thought *"I am going to fire her ghetto, two timing, back stabbing ass".*

Then she thought about it, she had to keep her cool, if she confronted Mona and was wrong about her, then Mona would know where Sheldon came from and whom she really was and things could get awkward after that. She decided to rip that letter up into tiny little pieces and flush it down the toilet and never even think about it again.

Sheldon was furious, she was so pissed that she had totally forgotten what time it was until the phone rang and startled her, she answered,

"Hello?"
"Yes hello, Mrs. Kingsland?" said the voice from the other end.

The voice continued on, "Mrs. Kingsland sorry to bother you, this is Mrs. Harper from Breckinridge Preparatory School, I am assuming that it slipped your mind that School was dismissed half a day today, so this is a friendly reminder to please come and pick Molly and Ashton up".
"Oh my God, I am so sorry Mrs. Harper, I will be there in less than twenty minutes" Sheldon frantically responded.

After hanging up the phone, Sheldon made sure that she properly discarded that God awful sorry attempt at an apology from her good for nothing mother. But as Sheldon grabbed her keys, purse and was putting Kayla's shoes on her feet, she felt the urge to use the bathroom.

"Hell I am already late getting the kids anyway, and if I do not go now, it might be another hour before I will be able to" Sheldon thought.

She ran up the stairs to use her and Chris' private bathroom, still toting little Kayla on her hip.

She sat on the toilet and after straining for about a good two minutes, barely anything came out. Even though her stomach was twisting and turning and cramping, it just wouldn't come out. She decided to just run get the kids and when she returned home, she would take a laxative, again.

She reached for the toilet paper, glancing into her bedroom to make sure that Kayla was still in the same spot she left her on the edge of her bed. Sheldon wiped and felt this warm liquid, she said to herself,

"I don't have diarrhea, so what could that be?" Sheldon glanced at the toilet paper, it was blood, dark, very dark, but it was blood all right.
"Damn" she said, "I have strained so much over the past couple of months that I have given myself hemorrhoids".
Sheldon washed her hands, grabbed Kayla and her purse and keys again, and jumped into her SUV and was off to fetch the kids.

Sheldon made a mental note to go ahead and make that doctor's appointment and at least get some hemorrhoid cream or something. She decided that this was something else she would not tell Chris about; this and that damn letter.

When she made it back she was surprised to find Chris at home.

"I left the office a little early so that we could make some martinis, put a couple of steaks on the grill and hang with the kids out by the pool".

Then he added in a much lower voice, "Sheldon, are you on your period *again?*" Sheldon looked up surprised and said, "no why would you ask me that sweetheart?"

"Well, I went to use the bathroom and there was a wad of bloodstained toilet paper on the floor behind the toilet seat. I am glad I found it and not Mona or one of the children, kinda embarrassing if you know what I mean."

Sheldon, thought to herself, *Oh shit, I was in such a hurry that I probably missed dropping the tissue into the toilet*, then she said aloud with a nervous chuckle, "well this is even more embarrassing sweetheart, but I think I might have hemorrhoids. I saw blood after I strained a little too hard while using the bathroom".

The look on Chris' face said it all, so Sheldon was not surprised when he firmly said, "Sheldon, no more excuses we are calling Dr. Braman right now!" Without even waiting for a response from her, he picked up the phone and dialed Dr. Phillip Braman's personal cell number. Even though he and Dr. Braman were not really close friends per se, they did enjoy a golf game together a few times a year.

"Hey Phillip, how are you doing? Look I know how busy you must be, but if you could squeeze in a few minutes today before you leave the office, I would be forever grateful. I need to bring my wife in immediately".

Even though Sheldon couldn't hear what Dr. Braman was saying on the other end, Chris continued, "Yes, yes I know she postponed her appointment a few months back, but there is an issue and I would like her to be seen as soon as possible". Silence........"Ok, I really appreciate you Phillip, see you around 5:30 then; thanks again, bye".

CHAPTER 12

Tests, What Tests?

Sheldon had no other choice; there was no arguing with Chris when his mind was made up. On their way across town to Dr. Braman's office they stopped at Chris' Aunt Rosa's to drop off the kids. Aunt Rosa was pretty much the only one in Chris' family who fully embraced and loved Sheldon unconditionally.

Rosa walked onto the porch, a short, plump woman with cotton white hair tied back in a tight bun, and kind smiling eyes; she bent down to hug the two older children and reached out to get Kayla from Chris' arms.

"My little angels" she exclaimed, "Come on in, Auntie just baked a fresh batch of cookies".

She had the children wave goodbye to their parents as they drove off.

When Chris pulled into the parking lot of the hospital, Sheldon started to feel a bit uneasy, "What if it is not hemorrhoids, what if it is something serious?"

For the first time in a very long time she started to feel a bit vulnerable and out of control.

Chris reassured her, "Honey this is just a precaution, look at you, you are perfect. How many women look like you after giving birth to three children? You eat right, you exercise, you do not smoke and you are virtually free of any stress in your life. Again Sheldon, this is just a precaution, Phillip will give you some special cream or something and probably tell you to eat more fiber and we will be on our way".

Sheldon placed her hand in her husband's and looked up and gave him a gentle kiss, and said to him "Thanks for easing my mind sweetheart, you always know how to make me feel better".

"When we leave here, we are going to go have some dinner and then pick the kids up" Chris added. They got on the elevator and Chris pressed the number four button to get to Dr. Braman's office.

After a brief wait in the cozy but way too sanitized waiting room, Sheldon was called back by a stern yet kind looking nurse.

She must be new Sheldon thought; *I really haven't been here in a long time.*

She was weighed and realized that she was 7 pounds down from her usual one hundred and twenty-five pounds. "Hmmmm" she mumbled, "I now weigh exactly what I did in high school and college".

After the usual blood pressure check and temperature check which all seemed pretty normal, she was informed that her blood pressure was a little elevated, but the nurse reassured her that it was probably the stresses of the day.

As Sheldon sat on the table in the waiting room trying to keep the cheap plastic gown closed, all sorts of awful things swam through her thoughts. When the nurse stuck her head inside the room to tell Sheldon that Dr. Braman was going to be in shortly, Sheldon asked her to please have her husband to come back to the room.

Dr. Braman entered the room with a smile for Sheldon and a handshake for Chris.

"So what is bothering you Sheldon? When Chris called, he sounded like this was an emergency".

Before Sheldon could respond, Chris blurted out,

"Phil, it seems like she was bleeding from her, well you know, when she went to do number two". Dr. Braman responded, "Really, tell me Sheldon have you been constipated lately where you had to strain to have a bowel movement?"

Sheldon thought *Oh hell, I have to be honest now.* "Yes, Doctor, for over a couple months now".

"WHAT?" Chris bellowed, "You haven't said a word to me about any of this". Dr. Braman saw that Chris was getting really worked up, even though it was out of concern, so he asked him to calm down.

Chris sat down in the chair, while Dr. Braman started to examine Sheldon. The doctor felt her neck, looked into the back of her throat, looked into her ears, listened to her heart and lungs; all the while with a steady frown on his face. Sheldon didn't really pay much attention to his face; she was looking at Chris's face. He seem so angry that he looked like he was about to cry.

Then Dr. Braman said, "I am going to check you for hemorrhoids now, do you want Chris to leave? If you do I can call the nurse back in". Of course she wanted Chris to leave, this exam was turning into more of an embarrassment than her yearly "stirrups" exam as she called it.

But she didn't do the latter, she told Dr. Braman that yes she wanted Chris to stay. Chris got up and walked around to be facing her as she awkwardly bent over the table for Dr. Braman to administer the "examination".

After Dr. Braman gloved and lubed up, he gently started to talk her through the procedure. Sheldon gritted her teeth and tried to think about being somewhere else, anywhere than there at that moment. The lubricating jelly the doctor used was a bit cold, and gooey and very unpleasant. After feeling around for a while, Dr .Braman told her to clean herself up and get dressed. He left with a promise to be back shortly.

Dr. Braman, finally came back into the room to find a fully dressed Sheldon seated next to Chris with him gently rubbing her back. Dr. Braman started by saying, "Sheldon, I am glad that you came to see me today; first of all, I don't see any reason for concern, I did in fact find a few small hemorrhoids.

What concerns me is that there are in no way large enough to cause much if any discomfort and they are definitely not the cause of your constipation. Furthermore, they are not bleeding. So moving forward, I am going to order a colonoscopy; please understand that this is just a precaution and to give all of us peace of mind".

Chris said, "Well if it is nothing to worry about, why order a colonoscopy doctor?"

"Chris this is just a routine test to rule out anything else and give you guys peace of mind. Her lymph nodes are a bit swollen and then there is the weight loss" added Dr. Braman. Sheldon chimed in, "Dr. Braman, I can explain the weight loss, I started taking more pilates classes and I have really cut back on my carbohydrate intake".

"My wife is the healthiest person I know Dr. I mean Phillip, she takes pride in her appearance and she does in fact treat her body like a temple".

Dr. Braman stated, "Look guys, I would not be a very good Doctor and definitely less than a friend if I didn't order this test, I want to make sure that Sheldon is alright; that is the reason why I am ordering the test. She will be just fine, again this is just a precaution, please understand that this has to be done.

Even though rectal bleeding may not be serious, one should never assume this to be the case. I have to rule out every possibility before I can send you on your way with peace of mind; both for you and for me. "

CHAPTER 13

Worried And Impatient

On the ride home Sheldon was very quiet, she knew that Chris was more than a little annoyed with her for not telling him about her recent issues with her bowels. It was not the highlight of her day to talk to her husband about such issues. Besides, this was exactly the reason she didn't want to tell him in the first place.

The doctor finds a few little hemorrhoids and all of a sudden a colonoscopy is ordered and her husband is upset at her. *Gosh, how did we get from zero to here so fast?* she thought. Chris had decided to cancel the dinner plans he had made and just pick the kids up and head on home. He said that he was going to whip the kids up a quick bite put them to bed and then he needed to talk to Sheldon.

She knew this was coming, and she could not stop it. *Why would I want to stop it?* she thought. *God, some women would kill to have a husband who wants to talk.*

When they arrived at Aunt Rosa's house to get the kids, they found that Aunt Rosa was very disappointed that they got back so soon.

" I thought you two were going to dinner afterwards, so I fixed the kids a little something to eat and we were just about to play a game of chutes and ladders" Rosa complained.

Chris leaned down to give her a kiss on the cheek and said, "thanks Auntie but things changed a bit and we are just going to go on home, but I promise you one afternoon next week we will drop them off and you can spend the entire afternoon feeding them junk and spoiling them rotten".

"Everything is ok isn't it?" Rosa asked after taking a look at both Chris and Sheldon's faces. Even though Sheldon's skin was significantly darker than Chris', you could still tell that she had gone completely pale and a bit ashen.

Rosa wasn't "born tomorrow" as she usually quipped, so when Chris assured her that everything was fine, she knew that he was either straight lying to her or he was covering something up. Either way, she got the feeling that now was not a good time to pressure them, and she hugged each of the kids and bid them all farewell.

As they drove into their prestigious gated community Chris glanced back and realized that both Molly and Kayla were already fast asleep. *No baths for them tonight* he thought. He knew that if he woke them up for their baths that it would be quite a while before they fell back to sleep.

So when they pulled into the garage, Sheldon took Kayla while Chris toted Molly straight up to their rooms and changed them into their pajamas. Meanwhile Ashton opted to take a bath and then sensing that his parents were not in the best of moods decided not to push his luck with any demands. He didn't even ask to be tucked in; he simply got into bed and tightly closed his eyes.

Sheldon went straight to her room and started to undress as soon as she hit the bedroom door. She just had to take a very hot shower; she felt dirty, and wanted to wash the entire doctor visit down the drain.

She was in the shower no more than two minutes when Chris stepped into the shower behind her. She turned and looked up at him with tears in her eyes and she then buried her face against his naked chest and let the tears flow. Chris knew better than to start talking to Sheldon at that moment. He knew in his heart that she was already on edge and feeling badly about not coming to him sooner. He did not want to push her further down than she already was at this moment. No, he couldn't do that, she was being hard enough on herself.

He place his hand under her chin and lifted her head up to look at him and when he looked into those soft brown eyes, his heart melted and he fell in love with her all over again. There were no words exchanged between them in the shower, as he bathed his wife with the utmost care, taking his time as he soaped every inch of her perfect body.

After so many years, words did not need to be exchanged between them, for his hands were familiar with every curve and crevice on her body. He leaned down and kissed her soft lips as though they were a delicate rose petal about to fall to the ground. As they left the shower and headed towards the bed, Chris realized that tonight was not about words or the height of passion or thrashing around under the covers.

Tonight was about holding his wife's naked body next to his and stroking her and caressing her to ease her fears and ease her mind; to make her feel safe and protected and to remind her that there was no other place in or out of this world he would rather be than right there holding her in his arms. As Sheldon's breaths indicated that she had peacefully fallen asleep, Chris couldn't help but let the unthinkable creep into his thoughts. *Suppose it is something more than just hemorrhoids, suppose it is something so awful that I end up losing my wife?*

Chris quickly pulled himself together and tried to allow happy thoughts to enter his mind. But this little voice kept nagging him over and over again, "What if….?"

Sheldon had already slipped into a very deep sleep. She didn't even budge when Chris kissed her on the forehead and whispered, "I love you" into her ear.

CHAPTER 14

I Do Not Like That Word

Anxiety took over Sheldon on the day before her colonoscopy. Not only was she not allowed to eat, but she had to drink a gallon of the most unpleasant tasting liquid you could ever imagine. She couldn't even leave the house, having to stay within close proximity of her bathroom at all times. She was *not* looking forward to this procedure at all.

Chris had arranged everything; he had picked up the prescription for the colon cleansing liquid she was taking, he had arranged for Aunt Rosa and Mona to stay overnight the day of the procedure. He figured that Aunt Rosa would be totally responsible for the kids while Mona took care of the household duties.

Everything was covered, he had also decided to take the day off, someone had to drive Sheldon to and from the procedure. Chris didn't have to be in court that day at all; even if he did, one of his other partners at the law firm would have had to fill in or the case moved to another date. Whatever it took, his wife came first.

As they drove to the medical facility the day of the dreaded colonoscopy, Sheldon closed her eyes and leaned her head on the headrest. She thought about the three kids and how much she loved them.

She even managed a slight smile as she thought about everything she was looking forward to; high school, graduations, first dates, weddings; yup she had a lot to look forward to with her children. And with Chris by her side, she knew that her life would continue to be perfect.

Next to her, Chris' thoughts were taking a different direction. He had so many questions for Sheldon once this was all over. Like was she ever going to forgive her mother and allow her to see the kids? What about her family medical history, is there anything that could affect their kids in the future? Is there anything in that medical history that is affecting her now? Is this something serious or life threatening?

They arrived about thirty minutes before Sheldon's scheduled time. Early enough for Sheldon to get the necessary paperwork done and get changed into the hospital gown. When she was placed on the table, all she remembered was Chris kissing her bye.

It seem like she had just closed her eyes briefly when she opened them again. She groggily asked when they were going to begin and was told that it was already done.

That was it? she thought, *I don't feel any pain or any discomfort or anything at all, just extremely tired.* When Chris came in to the room she repeated her thoughts to him. He was relieved to hear that she was not suffering any type of discomfort.

Sheldon managed a smile and said to Chris, "God I am starving". They both shared a laugh and without verbally acknowledging to each other, they were both relieved to put this behind them.

Chris told her that on the way home they would stop and he would get her whatever she felt like eating. He then added that the meal would be to take home of course.

He was aware that Sheldon was in no position physically or anesthetically to be seen out at a restaurant at the moment.

As Chris was assisting Sheldon in getting dressed, there was a knock on the door. Dr. Braman along with the other physician, Dr. Heisman who was the Proctologist entered the room. They did not seem to be on a mission of good will.

Chris and Sheldon greeted both physicians and thanked Dr. Heisman for doing such a great job. Chris then asked Dr. Braman what he was doing there.

"Dr. Heisman immediately called me in since I am not only your doctor Sheldon, but a friend".
"Wha, wha why, Dr. Braman, what is the matter, is there something wrong?" exclaimed Sheldon.
The doctors exchanged uncomfortable glances with each other, then Dr. Heisman nodded at Dr. Braman.

"Chris, Sheldon, first of all, do not be alarmed with what I am about to say to you." Dr. Braman then reached over and took Sheldon's chart from Dr. Heisman's hand and continued on.

"Dr. Heisman found not one but two seemingly large masses on your colon Sheldon. Even though we are extremely concerned by the looks and size of them, we are not anticipating anything really serious. Your age, overall health and medical history is in your favor."

By now Sheldon and Chris were in a fog, all they seem to have heard were the words "two large masses". Everything else that Dr. Braman said sounded like, "blah, blah, blah, blah".

Dr. Heisman picked up where Dr. Braman left off, "Mrs. Kingsland, I called Dr. Braman in because what I am about to tell you might change your life forever or it might not; either way, I felt like having him here might lighten what I am about to tell you".

By this time tears were flowing down Sheldon's face and Chris was squeezing her hand to tightly that it started to become painful.
Dr. Heisman continued, "Mrs. Kingsland, do you have a history of cancer in your immediate family?"

"Cancer, did you say cancer?" Sheldon tearfully asked.
"Please do not be alarmed Mrs. Kingsland, these are just mandatory questions I have to ask".
"Ok, ok will one of you please tell me what the hell is going on here? All of a sudden you all are talking about cancer?" Chris was pissed.

CHAPTER 15

In Shock

"Mr. Kingsland, finding two masses or tumors that size is almost unheard of in a woman your wife's age, so I am trying to rule out everything in theory before we do any other tests, that is why I am asking these questions.

We have to schedule surgery immediately to remove the tumors. Unfortunately, no matter what the tumors look like or seem like, we cannot accurately diagnose anything until they are biopsied".

Chris and Sheldon both looked as though they just found out that a massive asteroid was about to hit the planet earth and that earth would be completely annihilated in a couple of hours. That is how shocked and surprised they both were.

"So we do not know for sure that this is anything other than a couple of overgrown tumors, right?" Chris asked.

Dr. Braman answered, "Chris, we are hoping and praying that is what these are, but experience tells us different; we just have to hope for the best. I am going to schedule Sheldon's surgery as soon as possible; if the schedule permits, I want to go with the day after tomorrow".

"Did you say the day after tomorrow? That is too soon, I have so much to do, wha…" Chris did not let her finish her sentence, "Sheldon what you have to do is the least of our worries right now, let's just concentrate on you getting this surgery, and them finding that this is just a couple of benign tumors so that we can put all this behind us and get on with our lives".

Dr. Braman and Dr. Heisman exchanged knowing glances. They both seem to be already aware of what the surgery would reveal. But some things are better left unsaid.

Back at home Sheldon sat on the floor with all three of her children. She hugged and kissed them until they were pulling away from her. She could not help but wonder if she would die and leave her precious children.

Each time her mind wandered off like that, she had to remind herself that she was not even diagnosed with cancer, but yet she was already planning her own funeral.

Chris came and sat down next to her; he put his arm around her.

"We are going to beat this Sheldon; no expense will be spared to take care of you. I was upstairs calling my partner and my secretary; I have cleared my schedule for the next month and I have asked Aunt Rosa to help with the kids".

"But Chris, I will be fine, it is just surgery to remove the tumors".

"We do no know how long your recovery will take and I am not going to leave your side. The children must be cared for and you will need to be cared for as well".

Tears filled Sheldon's eyes and she looked at her husband and wondered what she ever did to deserve such a wonderful and caring man.

She held his face in her hands, and whispered, "Thanks Chris, everything will be fine, you will see honey, I will be back in my pilates class in a couple of weeks".

Chris leaned in and hugged his wife very tightly; he loved her so very much. As he hugged her, he looked up and said a silent prayer, *God, please do not take your angel back, I need her here with me.*

In preparation for her surgery, Sheldon did not have much time to get anything done. What she really wanted to do and she did, was spend some time with the kids. She knew that for at least a few weeks she would not be able to drive or do anything with them.

So she spent the next day taking them for ice cream, to the mall shopping and finally home to explain to them that mommy was having a little surgery and will be at the hospital for a few days. She explained to them that daddy was taking off work and that Aunt Rosa was going to be staying for a few days.

"Are you going to die Mommy?"
"No Ashton, why would you ask that?"
"Because you are going to the hospital, and people die in the hospital".

"No, you mustn't think that, yes some people do die in the hospital, but only people who are very, very sick. Mommy is not really sick, I just have a couple of things growing inside me that do not belong there, and the doctor is going to take them out".

"Do you promise not to die Mommy" Molly chimed in.
"Mommy promises not to die", Sheldon said, and gave Molly a big hug and a kiss.

Little Kayla was not paying them any attention, she had caught a glimpse of "Clifford The Big Red Dog" on the television and "Clifford" now had her full attention.

Once Mona came in the door, Sheldon decided to go to her room and get a bag all packed, and take a nice long relaxing bath. After surgery, it would be a while before would be able to took a bath.

As she sat in her jetted jacuzzi bathtub, she looked around and realized what a very privileged life she was blessed with. She could not help but wonder if maybe God had blessed her with so much so soon, because he knew that she wasn't going to be around long.

She pushed that thought from her mind, and quickly went back to appreciating all that she had; especially her husband and kids.

She then began to wonder how her mother was doing, something that she hasn't been concerned with for many years. She couldn't figure out how all of a sudden she wanted to know how her mother was doing.

Well, once I get out of the hospital and I am all healed and better, I might give her a call; just a call to say hello, nothing more, and certainly no visits.

As much as Sheldon wanted her mother to see how well she had done and how perfect her life was, she did not want her in her home. She did not want to suddenly be financially responsible for taking care of her mother and all her siblings as well. So even though she made a mental note to call her mother, she quickly decided against bringing her for a visit.

Not only was she afraid of what her mother might say to Chris, but she did not want her children getting attached to her.

When they arrived at the hospital early the next morning, Chris was a pillar of strength and positivity for his visibly nervous wife. As they wheeled her into the operating room, she had tears in her eyes; but when she looked up at Chris, he was smiling gently at her.

As soon as Sheldon's gurney disappeared from view, Chris broke down crying.

Across town, on the other side of the tracks, Mildred was on her knees leaning against her bed praying for her daughter's good health and recovery. Mona had been doing a great job of keeping her informed.

After what seemed like an eternity in the waiting room, Chris looked up and saw the doctor walking towards him. He jumped up, "Is my wife ok?"

CHAPTER 16

Bad News

"Mr. Kingsland, as soon as we opened your wife up, we immediately took a sample and sent it down to pathology. Unfortunately, I don't quite know how to say this, and there is no easy way of saying this, but your wife has colon cancer".

"Colon cancer?" Chris blindly sat back down; he was suddenly numb.
"Yes Mr. Kingsland, but there is more"
"More?"

"We discovered two more tumors on her liver. We didn't touch them, since we weren't prepared for something as delicate as liver surgery. At this point, we are saying that it is cancer as well.

The colon surgery was successful; we removed the tumor and also took out ten inches of colon that surrounded it.

She will have to have a colostomy bag for a few weeks until she heals. However, once she heals we are going to have to go back in a few months and remove those tumors from her liver.

Of course there is always chemotherapy, but we can wait to discuss treatment options once she has healed from this surgery."

Chris barely heard anything that Dr. Heisman said. He was suddenly in a fog; after the word cancer, he really hadn't heard much else.

"Mr. Kingsland, did you hear anything what I said?"

"Yes, Doctor; my wife has cancer?" Chris couldn't hold it back any longer, he broke down right there in the waiting room and sobbed like a lost child.

"When can I see her?"

"She is in recovery now, I will take you in there; and please Mr. Kingsland, do not mention any of this to your wife until she is out of recovery and in a room and we can both speak to her at the same time."

Chris walked into the room and saw his wife there, unconscious, looking frail and weak. He pulled a chair closer to her bed and took her hand and gently kissed it. "I love you Sheldon, you are my life".

Sheldon awoke to a nurse checking her pulse and Chris holding onto her other hand. She smiled at him and whispered, "it's all over, finally, we can get back to our normal lives now".

She knew her husband well enough to look at his face and know that something was just not right.

"Is something wrong Chris?"
"Just rest now sweetheart, we can talk later"
"Chris, what is wrong, is there something you are not telling me?"
"Sheldon, I just want you to rest right now, shhhhhh, don't try to talk"
"I am in a lot of pain, can you ask the nurse to please bring me something for the pain".
"Sure honey", as he pushed the button and told the voice on the other end that his wife needed something for her pain.
"Now tell me Chris, what is going on?"

The nurse came in and injected a dose of morphine directly into the intravenous line.

Chris was still searching for the right words or the right little white lie to tell Sheldon, when he glanced over and saw that the minute the medication hit her veins she was out like a light. He was saved, at least for now.

CHAPTER 17

Confronting Them

As Chris pulled out of the hospital's parking garage, he had tears in his eyes. He glanced up briefly and slammed his hand on the steering wheel, 'Why God, why?"

Before he could say anything else, his phone rang.
"Chris?"
"Mother?"
"Yes dear, Rosa told me about your wife"
Chris felt a lump in his throat as he gritted his teeth, "she has a name mother."
"How is Sheldon doing?"

Chris was an emotional mess, so much so that he pulled over to the side of the road and broke down in tears even more. "Oh mother, it is much worse than the doctors thought; not only is it cancer, but when they opened her, there were two more large masses on her liver.

Since they weren't prepared for such a delicate surgery as liver surgery, they just took a biopsy of both tumors, but did not attempt to operate on them".

"What?" Mrs. Kingsland exclaimed.
"Mother, my wife has cancer, not only in her colon but seemingly also on her liver; what am I suppose to do? Suppose something happens to her".
"Chris, first of all you need to calm down"
"Calm down? Why am I even telling you all this mother, you do not care anything about Sheldon anyway"
"Yes, I do, *we* do; years have passed, and we know how much you love your wife and regardless of the past, she is your wife, she *is* a Kingsland, and she is the mother of our grandchildren, so needless to say we are very concerned about Sheldon."

"Mother, don't bullshit me now, it is not the time ok?"
"Chris, why don't you come by here so that we can talk? Please, please, please say yes. Just come by; and can you bring the kids?"
"No mother" Chris responded.

There was a silence, then Chris added, "I will be there shortly, but I am not bringing the children; now is not a good time to have a family reunion".

Sitting in the library at his parents' house, Chris tried his best to compose himself. He knew that he needed to get this all out of his system now, because he had to be strong for Sheldon.

"Chris, how long did she have symptoms, or did she have any symptoms?" the elder Mr. Kingsland inquired.

"I am not sure dad, she had been using laxatives and colon cleansers for a while before I found out".
"See Chris, that is the problem with black people, they do not take care of themselves"

Chris looked up with contempt at his father, "don't you dare talk about my wife that way, whatever feelings or resentments or whatever it is you have against her race you are going to have to get over it.

Sheldon is my wife, and has been for a while, she is not going anywhere; and you have three grandkids who should be bouncing on your lap and being spoiled by you.

You chose to ignore all these good things and blessings because my wife happens to be black?"

By now Chris had gotten up from his seat and was towering over his dad, "I know that you come from a different time and place, but did you stop and think for one second that I love Sheldon and she is here to stay? If you want me to marry someone else, do me a favor, go and marry them yourself."

Years of buildup had led to this; Chris pointed over to his mother, "Both of you are hypocrites, you go to church every single Sunday and give to multiple charities and talk about how you are not racist because you have black friends, and Chinese friends and Hispanic friends.

But tell me, do any of these so called friends know that deep down inside that you all do not think of them as your equal?"

"Chris, how dare you speak to us this way and insult us in our own home?" his mother chimed in.

"Mom, just shut to hell up, I am sick and tired of sweeping this under the rug. Money does not give you the green light to be jackasses. I have dealt with this for too long now, the bottom line is, if you all are not genuine about your feelings and concerns towards my wife, then let me know; because if you are not then this will be the last time I set foot in this house, and the last time you will ever hear from me!"

By now Chris was sobbing, he sat back down and buried his head in his hands. His mother was the first to walk over and put her arms around him. "Chris, I don't know what to say, there is no excuse for our behavior".

Mr. Kingsland said, "Chris, whatever you need from us, we are here for you and no, I am not talking about money this time; you can count on us".

Once home, Sheldon was in a lot of pain; so much so that she did not want to get up and walk around like the doctors had advised. She wanted to hold and pick up her kids, she wanted go for a drive, she wanted to go shopping, and she wanted to make love to her husband.

She cried for the first few days, always when Chris was out of the room. She realized that had to pull herself together and put on a brave front, if she broke down, her family would suffer.

Prior to being discharged from the hospital, they had been a meeting with the doctors. Sheldon found out that she had what is called Adenocarcinomas, a very common type of colorectal cancer, so common, that in fact it accounts for 95% of all colorectal cancers. She could not wrap her mind around that information.

CHAPTER 18

HAUNTING REALITIES

By now Sheldon was becoming increasingly aware of her mortality. She had made the tough decision to endure chemotherapy, and had already scheduled her liver surgery.

During this time, she had cried almost everyday, making sure to never allow the kids or Chris to see her. She would cry until she hiccupped and until it physically hurt, repeating one phrase over and over again, "I want my mom, I want my mom".

Deep in Sheldon's heart, she wanted her mother to be there with her. Her mother had missed so much of her life; her graduation, her wedding, the birth of her three kids. Sheldon did not want to waste anymore time.

Now as she looked at herself in her bathroom mirror once again, the image was now a bit different. She was now down to barely one hundred pounds, her head was bald, and her skin had this grayish tint. Chris still told her everyday, how beautiful she was and how there was no other place he would rather be than right there with her.

Sheldon was seeing everything around her and everything in her life in a brand new light. Smells, shapes, the sun, the moon, even the grass gave her excitement. She came to the realization that sometimes you have to face death in order to live, to really live.

She made up in her mind that she was going to fight this cancer like she would fight the devil and she was going to live her life to the fullest.

She was going to appreciate everything she was blessed with. No, not her SUV or her closet filled with high end clothes, or her multimillion dollar house. She was going to roll around outside in the grass with her kids, she was going to find a beach and walk barefoot in the sand.

She was going to remind her husband everyday how much he meant to her. One more thing, she was finally prepared to forgive her mother; but why did it take death staring her in the face before she decided to do it?

CHAPTER 19

FORGIVENESS IS SO IMPORTANT

Mildred was sitting on her recliner waiting on the mail man. She was expecting her disability check in the mail and she couldn't wait. The light bill was almost $100 and she had to call and beg them to pay it in two installments to keep her lights on. The government use to pay that too, but once she was approved for disability she became responsible for it herself.

Yes, here he is, right on time.
"Morning Miss. Mildred, how's it going today?"
"Morning Calvin, I am making it, this old body not like it use to be"
"Got your check here for you, and a very nice looking envelope from a very expensive address across town."
"What?"
"Here you go Miss. Mildred, have a good day"

Mildred didn't even say goodbye to the mailman, she was too busy staring down at a handwriting that she had never forgotten. She was afraid to open it. Mona had told her all about Sheldoniqua's cancer and how it was eating away at her body. Mona had also told her that Sheldon was a much better person to work for now that she was battling cancer. She was kinder, more patient, more loving and seemed strangely happier.

Mom,

Where do I start? How are you? I am good, I am very blessed indeed, I have a husband who loves me, three beautiful children and a better life than I could have ever dreamed of.

First of all, I am sorry. God has a way of humbling us, of making us see what and who is really important in this life. I am just ashamed that it took cancer for me to really see how lucky and blessed I really am.

Even though I expect to live a very long time, I still feel the need to ask for forgiveness and more importantly to forgive. I am really ashamed to know that the woman who gave birth to me, is suffering while I am living in indulgence and abundance.

Mom, please forgive me, I am truly sorry for holding a grudge all these years. I wanted you at my graduation, but pride and stubbornness got in the way, I wanted you at my wedding, but again stupid pride, I wanted you to hold my hand when I was in labor and giving birth. Now that I am faced with the greatest test of my life and of my faith, I realize that I NEED you.

No matter how many spouses, or siblings or friends we have in this world, God blesses us with one mother who carried us for nine months and who bore the pain and agony of childbirth. No mother is perfect, but she is still in fact a mother. You are my mother and I love you.

You have three beautiful grandchildren, Ashton is now 12, Molly is 8 and little Kayla just turned 4. I cannot wait for you to meet them. I think Molly will remind you a lot of me when I was her age.

If you do not want to ever talk to me again, I completely understand, just know that I have no malice in my heart for you and I love you very much, and mom I do miss you.

I mailed this letter yesterday morning, and knowing that you would get it today, I am sending a car to pick you up at 2:00pm today to join us for dinner. Regardless of what you might have heard about us, there is no need for you to go out of your way to get all dressed up. I will be waiting at my window as I use to do when I was little; when I would wait to see you get off the bus on your way home from work.

I love you,
Sheldoniqua

By now Mildred could not control the tears that were now hitting the paper. All she could do was put her hand over her heart and cry. There were no words. She looked at the clock, it was almost noon. She realized that she had to start getting ready, she wanted to be ready when her ride got there.

Mildred looked up to the heavens and whispered, "Thank you Jesus, my daughter loves me".

CHAPTER 20

The Other Side Of The Tracks

A 1:55pm Mildred heard a knock on her door, a white man in a suit was standing there.

"I am here to take you to the Kingsland residence mam."

"Oh, thank you, a white driver, wow".

As the driver held the door open for Mildred to get in, she couldn't help but wonder what her neighbors were thinking.

She had a knot in her stomach and a million questions on her mind, would her grandchildren like her? Would her son-in-law resent her? Would they laugh at her old clothes and shoes?

After several miles of driving in complete silence (the driver obviously was not the talkative type), they pulled up to this huge gate with a sign that said 'MONTHAVEN'.

"Oh my Lord, I have heard of this place, there are no houses in here that are less than 5 million dollars" Mildred exclaimed. "My daughter lives *here*?"

The driver checked in at the gate and they swung open; Mildred's mouth dropped and remained that way. The houses were so magnificent, she was stunned, they all looked like the houses from the movie The Stepford Wives, not the original, the recent one with that Australian actress, Nicole something, whatever her name was.

They drove for several blocks and then they turned onto a circular driveway into what could not even be called a house. Mildred gasped in amazement at the monstrous Mediterranean style white and pale yellow home of her daughter.

As they pulled up, this frail looking woman with no hair and no shoes ran outside. At first Mildred thought they had the wrong house, then she recognized her almost unrecognizable daughter.

"Mom" Sheldon cried as she ran to the car and swung the door open.
"Sheldoniqua?" was all Mildred could say.

They held each other for what seemed like an eternity with nothing but tears being spoken between them.

When they finally pulled apart, Mildred asked, "Is this your house, do you really live here?"

"Yes, and with you here now, it seems to mean so much more to me"

"How many garages you got"
"Only a six car garage mom; come on in, you are embarrassing me"

Sheldon turned to thank the driver, she then took her mom's arm and led her through the front door.

The first thing that greeted Mildred was the double winding marble staircase that seemed to go on forever. The huge "K" that was in the floor was about 6 feet in height and just as wide.

Mildred had to compose herself, she started to take her shoes off, but her daughter told her to not worry about her shoes and to come into the kitchen so they could get something to drink.

As they walked into the kitchen, Mildred couldn't help but notice that it was maybe twice the size of her entire house.

She was seated for no more than a minute when a door that obviously led to the laundry room opened up. In walked Mona, with a laundry basket on her hip. She took two steps, looked up and almost dropped the basket of clothes she was holding.

"Mona, I am sure you know Mildred, my mother".

"Yes, ummmm, I do, yes I do know Mildred, hi Mildred". Mona was starting to stutter.

"Mona, would you pour us some lemonade and club soda with crushed ice, and fix a light snack for my mother before you start on dinner?"

Mona was still in the same spot. She was dumbfounded and very uncomfortable; so Sheldon *did* know all along that she knew Mildred.

"Mona, did you hear me?"
"Yes, Mrs. Kingsland, I did"

Mildred started to get up, "no, no, I can fix my own stuff, Mona don't have to wait on me, we are neighbors for god's sake, I am nobody important".

"Mom, please sit down, you are now a guest in my home, as a matter a fact you are not even a guest, my home is now your home; this is Mona's job, please let her do her job".

Mildred sat down but she was very uncomfortable with Mona waiting on her hand and foot.

In Mona's mind, she was fuming, w*hy the hell do I have to wait on and serve my poor, ghetto ass neighbor? She aint got shit and all of a sudden her daughter get a conscience and I got to serve she? If I did not need this job, I would quit right now.*

Mona smiled politely as she placed the drinks on the counter and turned to make the sandwiches.

There was silence, Sheldon decided to wait until they were through eating and upstairs before she talked to her mother openly. She did not trust Mona.

CHAPTER 21

THIS IS NOT A HOUSE

After the light snack, Sheldon took Mildred on a tour of the house. Mildred was in total awe of the way her daughter lived. "Wow" was all she kept muttering to herself; the place was like an apartment complex. She still couldn't figure out why any one family needed eight bedrooms and ten bathrooms.

Sheldon saw the look on her mother's face and realized that this should have been done a long, long time ago. She took her through the kids' room, to the workout room, to the movie theater room and finally to the master bedroom. Mildred could not believe Sheldon and her husband's bedroom; one word, spectacular.

There king size bed sat in the middle of the room at the top of three steps. The entire room looked like something from one of those Ethan Allen commercials on television.

Dark blue with trims of baby blue and pure white was everywhere. Sheldon's closet was like the better dresses department at Macy's. When they walked through, Mildred was afraid to touch anything, there was even a television in Sheldon's closet.

And the shoes, oh the shoes; Mildred started to count the pairs of shoes, but she quit after the sixtieth pair. A far cry from the one pair, she afforded Sheldon when she was a little girl.

"Sheldon, how can you all afford all this, what does your husband do?"
"Mom, he is an attorney, a corporate attorney, actually an owner/partner in the law firm"
"I didn't know lawyers made this much money; are you sure that he isn't doing something illegal?"
"Mom, even if my husband never worked a day in his life, we would still be able to live like this; his trust fund money alone could support us, our children, our great grand children and still have plenty to spare."

Sheldon added, "Chris works because it is his passion to work as an attorney, not because he ever needs to".

Before Mildred could respond, voices came from downstairs.

"Mommy, mommy where are you?"

Sheldon started smiling, "Chris is home with the kids, come on downstairs and meet everyone".

They started down the stairs, but was met halfway by three of the most beautiful children that Mildred had ever laid eyes on.

“Mommy, who is this?” leave it up to Molly to get straight to the point.

“Let’s all go back downstairs into the living room and I will introduce you” said Sheldon.

They all followed Sheldon into the living room and sat down.

“Chris, honey please join us in the living room, there is someone here I want you to meet” Sheldon yelled around the corner.

About 30 seconds later a white man with dark hair and deep set dark brown eyes appeared at the door. The man was straight out of one of those cologne commercials, Mildred thought.

He walked into the room and his attention went straight to his wife; he bent down and hugged and kissed her and told her how beautiful she looked.

He sat on the arm of the chair Sheldon was sitting in, placed his arm around her shoulder and he did not budge.

“Chris, kids there is someone here that I want you to meet. This is something that I should have done years ago. Chris, Ashton, Molly, Kayla, meet Mildred Morrison; my mother”.

CHAPTER 22

IS IT GRANNY OR GRANDMA?

The room went silent, but Molly, never one to stay quiet for too long was the first to speak, "You are my grandmother, really?" She got up and ran over Mildred and gave her a great big hug. The other kids followed.

Chris, even though stunned, never missed a beat, he stood right up and walked right over and hugged Mildred.

"So very nice to meet you, this is long overdue; what a pleasure this is".

Sheldon was surprised and relieved that Chris handled it so well, and was very impressed at the loving, accepting nature of her children. She sat there with her hands clasped together with her thumbs touching her nose with tears flowing down her cheeks.

"Is grandma going to live with us?" Ashton asked.

"Where did she live before?" Molly joined in.

"Ok kids, give your grandmother some breathing room" Sheldon answered.

Nobody noticed how quiet Chris had become; his mind was racing, why all of a sudden is Sheldon clinging to her mother? For God's sake in all the years they had been married, talking about her mother was the one taboo that stood between them.

He couldn't help but wonder if maybe Sheldon felt like she was dying, and suddenly wanted to make peace with her mother. Whatever the reason, he needed to talk to his wife.

Chris' mind continued to race and the more his mind raced the angrier he got. How could Sheldon be so selfish, towards the kids, towards him? Why did she spring her mother on them? Now there is going to have to be a lot of explaining to do to the children. You just don't do a magic trick and make a grandmother appear out of thin air. This should have been discussed. Chris felt like he was ambushed. Plain and simple.

CHAPTER 23

IT ALL FALLS DOWN

Chris arrived at work in a fog. He sat down at his desk and with each passing thought he got angrier and angrier. Chris had always been the flagship of husbands; after seeing his parents' business agreement of a marriage, he wanted his own marriage to be different.

He lost a lot of friends and some family members when he decided to spend the rest of his life with Sheldon. What was it about her? She was everything he ever wanted and desired. He had never imagined his life without her; until now.

"Mr. Kingsland?"
Chris looked up to a beautiful, sophisticated looking blond woman staring down at him.
"Yes, can I help you?"
"I am the new Temp here for this week while your assistant Mary is on vacation. I was here a couple days last week to train."
"Oh, where are my manners, I am so sorry, Maxine right?"
"Yes sir, let me know if there is anything I can do for you"

Chris couldn't help but notice how sexy this young woman was, she looked no more than 23 or 24, probably right out of college.

His mind returned to his wife; he wanted to talk to Sheldon about her mother. But he couldn't help but glance over to Maxine whose legs were now crossed revealing a hint of a view of her black garter belt. *Didn't know women still wore those things* Chris thought. Then he scolded himself for finding pleasure in what was right in front of his eyes.

He thought of his wife, so fragile, yet so strong. The mother of his children, the woman whom he really did forsake all others for. They had everything, how could God allow this to happen to them?

Chris sighed, cleared his mind and got up and walked over to Maxine, "I am heading out for a moment, please take any messages and if it is very important then just forward the call to my cell phone."

"Ok, Mr. Kingsland, will do."

Chris wondered if she could tell that he had been staring at her. Oh well, at least I still know that I am a red blooded man.

He thought that he was heading home, but instead he went to the coffee shop on the corner to sit and think in hopes of gathering his thoughts and clearing his mind.

Sheldon had about two more rounds of chemo left, he wondered if she could endure it. She had already lost a considerable amount of weight, and that damn cancer was spreading more rapidly than a forest fire on a hot, rainless summer day.

What would he and the kids do? How was he going to raise the 3 kids all alone; he certainly wasn't going to be looking for a new wife. Sheldon was irreplaceable. But he had to face reality; unless there was some kind of medical miracle, his beloved wife will not live to see any of their children even graduate from high school.

She did not even want to continue the chemotherapy, complaining that it made her much worse. He thought that she would want to do everything in her power to stay alive; why would she stop the chemo?

Chris had asked her that question over a week ago, and she replied that her body was tired, that she was tired and that she has turned everything over to God to handle. She did not want to discuss it any further. Then her mother had arrived.

He still had a million and one questions about her mother and about her complete change of heart.

Chris realized that he had been the best husband that he could be, and did not have one ounce of guilt in that department; so why all of a sudden was he starting to feel inadequate?

He had begged and pleaded with her to continue chemotherapy, at least do it for the kids. But Sheldon was adamant that she wanted to stop. Period.

He felt helpless, time was running out and there was nothing he could do about it. He had already pleaded with the doctors to convince Sheldon to continue treatment, he had consulted with top doctors on every continent and he had prayed more in the last month than he had all his life combined. The answers were all the same, unless she continued the chemotherapy, she probably had less than five months left to live.

CHAPTER 24

NOT ENOUGH TIME

Sheldon knew that time was running out. All of a sudden she had a multitude of things she wanted to do and say. She was quick to embrace her mother and let her back into her life, but she still had some things to say to her. Things she wanted to get off her chest.

She had spent weeks bargaining with God to grant her one single wish; to live long enough to see her children at least graduate high school. As much as she prayed, she knew it was one pray that was not going to be answered. The odds were clearly against her.

The chemotherapy was hastening her to the grave. She just knew it. It weakened her; it was meant to attack the tumors but instead she felt like it was slowly breaking her weak body down even more. Chris had tried his best to convince her to continue, but she refused. He was not the one to suffer, she was; and she was clearly suffering more with the chemotherapy than without it.

Sheldon spent many nights awake staring at the ceiling, pain resonating throughout her entire body. She began to reflect over her life. When she gave birth to her three children, she knew that she was going to be around to see her grandchildren. Sheldon finally came to the realization that there was only one person in control, and it was certainly not her.

Was God punishing her for living a lavish lifestyle all these years while her own mother, her flesh and blood, lived like a pauper? Surely not, she worked hard and deserved everything she had. It was not her fault that her mother chose the path she did and ended up with nothing.

Sheldon picked up the phone and called Mildred.

"Mom?"
"Sheldoniqua?"
"um yes, please mom, just call me Sheldon"
"How you feeling? Ya sound weak"
"I am doing good mom, I decided to stop the chemotherapy and just use my energy to spend time with my husband and the kids".
"Sheldoni…I mean Sheldon, why you do that? De chemo suppose to help you; aint it suppose to make the tumors smaller?"
"Yes mom, but while it is doing that, it is slowly killing other parts of my body as well. Tell me mom, please try to remember, do you have the slightest idea who my father is?"
Silence.
"Mom are you there?"
"Yes, I still here."
"Well?"

"Sorry Sheldon, I don't have a clue; why do you want to know after all these years?"
"Because mom, I want to know my family history, I want to know if I have or had a grandmother, an aunt, even a sister or brother who suffered from this disease."
"Oh, I sorry Sheldon"
"Could you please maybe *try* to remember?"
"Sheldon, if I could I would, but that was a long time ago and half the men I been with, I never knew or even met any of their family members".

Sheldon took a deep breath, and resolved to leave it alone. She felt like she was desperately grasping at straws now. Even if she got that information, it would be of no help to her at this point. Her weight continued to plunge, her once beautiful hair was now completely gone, her cheekbones were protruding; even her breasts had lost all their elasticity and looked like two withering pomegranates. She tried hard not to let Chris see her naked, she looked horrible. But somehow Chris always told her how beautiful she was. She knew he was being kind.

CHAPTER 25

BACK TO BASICS

Chris arrived home to find Sheldon in bed weeping. Her blood shot eyes spilling tears onto the pillow. He rushed over to her, but she pushed him away screaming,

"Get away from me Chris"
Chris was shocked, what did he do? What had happened between this morning and now?
"Sheldon, wha wha what's the matter?"
"What's the matter? You know what's the matter" Sheldon screamed.
Chris was speechless, he had never seen his wife like this, ever, not even while she giving birth.

"Sheldon, please tell me what's going on, did the doctor call? What is wrong?"

"Let me tell you what is wrong Chris, my whole life I had to fight to do better, to be better. I had to put up with my mothers' boyfriends touching me, I had to put up with living under horrible conditions, I had to put up with sisters who hated me simply because they thought I was prettier. I had to put up with many, many nights of studying my brains out just to get a scholarship to get out of that hell hole I was living in.

I had to put up with being looked down on by your friends, by classmates, by coworkers, and worse, by your parents Chris. I had to put up with stares and nasty comments throughout our entire marriage. I had to put up with seeing you estranged from your parents because of me. I had to even put up with you losing friends *and* family over me, over me. And for what Chris, for what? I am dying, and every single thing was in vain, every single thing was in vain Chris.

Hell, I even went through childbirth for nothing, I am not even going to see any of my children grow up. I bet your parents are going to be real happy when I am gone, cause now you can marry you a 'white as the driven snow' woman. What are you going to do about the kids Chris, tell people you adopted them?"

By now Sheldon was hysterical, and almost screaming. Chris listened with mouth wide open, in astonishment and disbelief.

"Sheldon, I am married to you because I love you and I chose you, just like you chose me. I don't care about anybody else or anything else. You walk around acting like you are the only one hurting. Sheldon, we are all suffering too."

"Who else is suffering Chris, I am the one with cancer, remember?"

"How could I forget Sheldon, you have given up, everyone is fighting for you but you. You act like you are already dead, yes

I said it; you act like you are already dead. Sheldon you are still in the land of the living; you still have kids who need you, you have a husband who needs you.

You are loved more than you could ever imagine, but you are too selfish to even see that. All you can see and focus on are the negatives. Fuck the past Sheldon. You cannot change it, if I had the power I would change the past for you, so that you would only have good memories.

Do you have any earthly idea how much I love you? How much our children love you? I am beginning to think that you only think about you?"

"Chri, Chri..."

"Shut up Sheldon, it is my turn now, let me finish. Not one time during our marriage or any pivotal moments in our lives have you ever wanted your mother around. All of a sudden you feel this need to satisfy some type of guilt or whatever the hell is going on in your head and you out of the blue spring her on me and the children.

Didn't you stop to even think that maybe the kids would have benefited from knowing their grandmother way before now? Did you even stop to think about the ramifications and the confusion you placed on our kids? Did you even think that maybe it could have been discussed with me first?"

Now it was Sheldon's turn to sit there with her mouth open.

"Sheldon, you think that just because you grew up poor that your life was somehow worse than mine simply because my family had money? Just because I refuse to dwell on the past and I choose to live in the here and now doesn't mean that I had a perfect life.

If you were not so busy feeling sorry for yourself and being the victim, you might have seen or even inquired about my pain or even your mother's pain. While you were busy living, your mother was busy slowly dying.

Have you stopped for one minute Sheldon and asked yourself that maybe your mother was going through hell all these years.

Your mother did the best she could with what she had and obviously her best wasn't good enough for you; so what? Get over it and move on. You cannot change anything Sheldon, the only thing you can change is the way you choose to deal with it.

So tell me are you going to spend your precious time living in the past and continuing to be a victim or are you going to live and fight this with everything in you?"

Sheldon couldn't respond. She knew that Chris was right. She never saw it that way before, she only looked at her own pain and suffering, never stopping to inquire about anyone else. Had she been really that selfish?

"One more thing Sheldon, don't you *EVER* even think, or even breathe a word again, implying that the birth of our children was in vain!"

CHAPTER 26

LAST CALL

Sheldon cried herself to sleep, knowing that her husband was right. She kept asking herself over and over again if she had really been so blind all these years.

Maybe she was so busy proving everyone wrong, including her own mother, that she truly lost sight of what was really important. After she had tucked all three children into bed, she had gone to the bathroom to talk to God. She prayed for forgiveness, she prayed for understanding and then she prayed again for God to spare her life so that she could live the way she was suppose to be living all these years.

Isn't it amazing that when we are dying is when we are closest to actually living?

Sheldon decided that she was going to live life to the fullest and if God by some chance didn't answer her prayers, at least she would die with no regrets.

She woke up at around 2:30 am.

"Chris, wake up, honey please wake up"

"What Sheldon, wha what's wrong?"

"Chris, remember last week you asked me what I wanted to do most, to just tell you and you would do it?"

"Yes, Sheldon, what is it; it is late"

"Chris, I know that you do not want to hear this, but I feel like I don't have much time left, and I honestly feel like I haven't been living at all."

"Sheldon, let's just talk in the morning, ok?"

"No, no Chris, please listen to me. I have decided what I want."

"Ok?"

"Chris, I want to go on a second honeymoon"

"Really? You just tell me where and I will take care of it tomorrow"

"I want to go back to Barbados".

"Really Sheldon?"

"Yes, only this time I want the kids and my mother to come with us"

"Sheldon, are you serious?"

"Yes Chris, that is my wish".

"Done."

The next morning bright and early, Sheldon got up with more energy than she had in a long time; maybe because her conscience was much lighter.

Chris had left her a note telling her that if she really wanted her mother to accompany them on the trip that she needed to call her as soon as possible and arrange for her to get a passport in a hurry. Sheldon knew that her mother probably didn't even know what a passport was.

So Sheldon, with her new burst of energy, decided to drive all the way to the other side of town, to a place that she hadn't seen in over ten years, and had intentionally blocked from her memory.

When she pulled her Audi in front of her mother's place, she knew that she was getting plenty of stares but she didn't think that anyone would recognize her. No, pre-cancer Sheldon maybe, but definitely not now since she had changed so much in recent months.

She had called ahead, so Mildred was on the porch waiting for her. She seemed kind of surprised to see Sheldon driving.

Sheldon waved to her, and she walked down the steps and got into the SUV.

“Mom, I am taking you to get a passport”

“A passport? for what?”

“Because we are taking you to Barbados with us”

“Barbados? Is that in the Bahamas?

Sheldon couldn’t help but chuckle a bit.

“No mom, it is an island in the Caribbean, it stands all on its own, and it is not in the Bahamas”.

“Can we drive there?”

Sheldon’s chuckle turned into laughter.

“Mom of course not, you cannot drive there”.

“Sheldon, I don’t think I can get on one ‘a dem planes”.

“Come on, I think you would enjoy it mom, plus I really want you there”.

“But Sheldon, I never been on a plane, I never even went to a airport”.

“Mom please, I never asked you for anything, please just do this for me”.

“Sheldon, I live this long to get killed in a plane crash?”

"No mom, look if you are that nervous, we will take you to the doctor to get some type of medication to calm your nerves during flight"

"Ok, ok, I will do it, but make sure I get some medication.'

Sheldon smiled and she headed to have Mildred's passport photos made and then on to the post office to apply for the passport.

Sheldon had a million things to do before the trip; she used her sudden burst of energy wisely. She called the school and advised them of the kids being taken out for the upcoming trip. She had to stop the mail, call the pediatrician to ensure that all the kids' shots were up to date, pack, take Mildred shopping; her list of things to do seemed to be never ending.

The kids were excited to have their mother back. They knew that mommy was sick, but bless their little hearts, they had no idea how sick.

Sheldon decided that she would explain it to them once they got back from Barbados.

Everything went according to plans. Mildred, visibly nervous went through everything like a pro. Even though everything was new to her, she listened and did everything she was supposed to do, right down to being patted down by a very manly looking woman at the Miami airport.

CHAPTER 27

SUNSET

Mildred thought that she had died and gone to heaven. She had slept through the entire almost four hour flight from Miami to Barbados (Sheldon was right, the medication worked wonders). When they landed at the Grantley Adams International Airport, Mildred got off the plane in complete awe; on the tarmac, she looked back up at the aircraft with mouth wide open. She could not and really did not even want to understand how something so big and so heavy could actually stay up in the air.

The airport was breathtaking, with luscious green plants everywhere and smiling faces greeting everyone. The kids were excited, and Sheldon actually had a smile of contentment on her face. Most of the commute through the airports were done with her in a wheelchair, but Sheldon didn't mind, she was surrounded by the people she loved most.

After they cleared customs, collected their baggage and found the driver to take them to their hotel, Sheldon started to lean heavily on Chris. She also seemed to be very short of breath. Mildred started to panic, but Chris reassured her that Sheldon was just tired from all the travelling. He told Mildred that once they got to the hotel, he was going to have Sheldon take a long nap while he took the kids down to the beach to play.

"Not a chance Chris, I am not missing anything, yes I am tired, but I can sit on a beach chair and watch you guys. If I get too tired, I will just nap right there on the beach."

The drive to their hotel was not too far at all; the first thing that scared the shit out of Mildred was that they were driving on the wrong side of the road. At first she thought that maybe the driver was drunk or something, until she realized that if that was the case, then *everyone* was drunk, because everyone was driving on the wrong side of the road. That was going to take some getting use to.

At the Sandy Lane hotel, they were greeted by a very pleasant brown skinned woman who welcomed them in a very deep accent. The accent, even though unmistakably Caribbean, had a very proper flair to it. She introduced herself as Monica and told them that if they needed anything at all to let her know. She wished them a wonderful stay and pointed out a few places of interest to visit while they were enjoying her beautiful island paradise.

Monica noticed that the younger woman looked painfully thin, and in her outspoken yet innocent Barbadian way, she commented that, "a few days here mam, and we are going to fatten you right up with some good Bajan food".

"Bajan?" asked Mildred

Chris cut in, "that is the local term for the people and the way of life Mildred, Bajan is actually short for Babadian".

"I guess you are the expert then sir, you are correct" said Monica.

"Oh, I am no expert Monica, we were here on our honeymoon years ago, and once the decision was made to come here, I made myself familiar with the culture from A to Z. And by the way, I cannot wait to have some of your um what you call it again? Yes, yes, macaroni pie. I think the kids are going to love it."

After checking in and changing the kids into more comfortable clothes, they all headed back downstairs to take a first walk on the beach. The kids were fascinated, Mildred was intrigued. She thought that she had died and went to heaven.

Sheldon was starting to feel horrible and the pain she was starting to feel was becoming unbearable. She whispered to Chris that she was nauseous and was feeling very, very bad. Chris had the oncologist on speed dial. He stepped away from everyone and dialed the doctor's number.

"Dr. Hill? Good to hear you, this is Chris, Sheldon Kingsland's husband".

"Yes, Chris, how are you, and more importantly, how is Mrs. Kingsland?"

Chris went on to explain that Sheldon wanted to travel to Barbados, where they had spent their honeymoon, but she seemed to be taking a turn for the worse. Dr. Hill told Chris that the only thing left for them to do was to make her as comfortable as possible.

He went on to tell Chris that he would not have taken her on such a long journey, but if that is what she wanted and if he was in Chris' place, he probably would have done the same thing. Dr. Hill advised Chris to give her the recommended dosage of Morphine if she got too uncomfortable. Chris, knowing that Sheldon did not want any pain medicine, thanked the doctor anyway. Dr. Hill said one last thing, "Chris, I am so very sorry".

That first night on the island was fun for everyone; Sheldon managed to smile and keep up a very brave front, for her mother, her husband, but most of all for her kids. They were having such a great time.

The next day Sheldon decided to stay in and just sit on the balcony looking out onto the ocean. The others had gone on a submarine ride. Sheldon had insisted they go without her, and it was like pulling a damn tooth to get Chris to leave her alone.

"I am just going to enjoy the scenery and rest up a bit Chris, so please, please go without me; I insist".

What Sheldon really wanted was to see the beautiful sunset all by herself. She knew that she didn't have many left and she wanted to enjoy them while she still could.

She sat there and watched the orange ball in the sky slowly make its way towards the horizon. Sheldon commented to herself aloud, "if I only knew how short my life was going to be, I would have enjoyed a whole lot more sunsets". With that, tears filled her eyes as she watched the sun become one with the ocean and slowly disappear, leaving an abundance of color on the horizon, and a calm like no other.

Sheldon exhaled deeply and then started crying. She really didn't know why she was crying. But the longer she cried, the more it became apparent that she was actually mourning her life. How many times had her kids called her to look at a picture they had made and she had brushed them off? How many times had that same sun set in Tennessee and she paid it no attention? How many times had she gone to bed angry for one reason or another? How many opportunities had she missed to be charitable, but wasn't?

Thinking back it wasn't because she was a selfish, mean spirited person; it was because she felt like she had all the time in the world. She just knew that they would be many more pictures that her kids would make, and many more sunsets to see. Why did she even for one minute think that she had any control over time at all?

CHAPTER 28

FREEDOM IS A KISS

On the third day of their vacation, Sheldon woke up feeling panicked. She could not explain it; she was panicked and calm at the same time. She panicked because she felt like she had a million things to do before……., but before what? And she was calm because she had talked to God and made peace within her heart.

Chris noticed that his wife had a far away look on her face. He was not stupid; as much as he wanted to deny it, he knew the end was near. Sheldon called each of her kids one by one and talked to them. Chris couldn't hear what she was saying, but the look in her eyes said it all.

She is saying her goodbyes he thought. A lump formed in his throat and stayed there. Sheldon refused anything to eat. Chris asked her if she wanted him to call a private jet to take them home, but she would not hear of it.

"I am in paradise Chris, there is no place I would rather be. I feel closer to God when I am here".

That afternoon Sheldon looked at Mildred, and said to her, "Mom, I love you and don't you for one minute ever forget that".

Mildred was dumbfounded, "Sheldoni, I mean Sheldon, I love you too and will, no matter what".

"Mom, you can call me Sheldoniqua, that is after all, my name. We can run, but there comes a time when the running stops and you have to face everything head on. I ran from my name all my life; I didn't even know why. But I shouldn't have, because in the end the only thing I really and truly do have is my name".

Sheldon asked Mildred if she could take the kids for a long walk on the beach, so that she could talk to Chris alone. As soon as Mildred and the kids left, Sheldon asked Chris if he could take her down to the beach. Chris was hesitant; hesitant and afraid.

"Why Sheldon? we can sit right here on the balcony and talk".

"No Chris, I want to go sit on the sand".

By now, Sheldon's voice was barely a whisper. Chris was numb.

But he granted her wish. What she didn't know was that Chris had already made arrangements for a private jet to transport them back home. He felt like Sheldon needed to be in the hospital receiving medical care.

Chris helped his now almost unrecognizable wife out onto the beach. He could feel the stares and hear the whispers. But he kept going.

When they got down onto the sand, Sheldon whispered, "right here Chris, right here".

She had chosen a spot that seem to be in direct line with the now setting sun.

Chris sat behind Sheldon and had her to lean back onto his chest.

"I love you more than life itself Chris; you have shown me more love than I could have ever dreamed of".

"Sheldon, come on sweetheart, let's just enjoy the sunset, so that I can get you back to the room."

"Chris, please promise me one thing".

"Anything Sheldon, anything"

"Promise me that you will never allow my children to forget about me".

"Sheldon, no, please don't talk like that"

"And please take care of my mother, and make sure that she spends lots of time with the kids, I think they can learn a lot from her".

Chris looked up; the sun seemed to be setting at a faster pace than it should.

Sheldon was now breathing like it took all her strength to push her chest out.

"Sheldon, please don't leave me, you are my best friend; please don't".

Sheldon turned her head around and up, she looked into Chris' eyes and whispered, "Kiss me baby".

Chris leaned down and kissed his wife amidst tears. In all their time together, it was the sweetest and most meaningful kiss they had ever shared. Sheldon gently pulled away and turned her head towards the horizon. As the sun set, Sheldon squeezed her husband's hand, closed her eyes and slightly gasped. By the time Chris looked up again, the sun had all but disappeared, and Sheldon hung lifeless in his arms. He remained there for what seemed like an eternity rocking back and forth with tears soaking his shirt. He did not want to move; for he knew that if he moved from that spot that reality would immediately set in.

WHERE AM I?

Sheldon looked up; Chris was no longer sitting behind her. Instead, there were three strange women all looking confused and another woman was making her way towards them.

She was still sitting on the sand, but not on the same beach in Barbados; and these women, who were they?

Some names shot out; Brea, Alex, Megan and then there was the other woman. The one named Megan seemed to know who the fifth woman was. Megan let out a muffled scream.

PART 2 – MEET MEGAN

The Great Pretender

"You stupid, short, fat bitch!" Megan was awaken by her husband's drunken rant once again. She was already nursing a sprained wrist and one of many black eyes that she had gotten over the past five years; she couldn't take anymore tonight, "please God, not tonight she prayed". She glanced at the clock by her bed, it was 11:00pm; "why God, why?" she pleaded silently.

Her husband stumbled into their bedroom, walked over to the bed and yanked the covers off of her. "Take that off and spread your legs" Bill grunted. He smelled of stale whiskey and seafood vomit.

Megan, with tears falling onto the pillow quietly said, "Bill, I ca-ca—can't tonight, it is that time of the month". Megan knew better than to say that, but it came out before she could stop herself.

Her thoughts went back four years ago when Bill forced himself on her even after she told him that she was on her period. Unfortunately she was wearing a tampon; but he didn't care.

Her screaming seem to have gotten him off, because the more she fought and screamed the more aroused he became. After that incident, she ended up at the emergency room in so much pain that she was vomiting and convulsing.

Megan had lied to the nurse and the doctor and told them that she had forgotten that she was wearing a tampon and that it was her own clumsy fault.

She also told them that the swollen lips and nose were from another clumsy encounter; with her bathroom door.

As Megan reached down to take her panties off, she knew that this was going to be another painful night for her. Since that night with the tampon incident, she had not gone to another female examination.

She was ashamed and afraid; her vaginal area resembled a war zone; or a cross between a sliced up piece of raw liver and a molding piece of swiss cheese. It had been bitten, cut, sliced, pinched and other things so horrendous that when she thought about them she literally threw up.

How did she end up like this? Megan had no idea either. She turned her head to the side as her tears continue to soak the pillow. Bill climbed on top of her; he huffed and puffed on top of her for what seem like an eternity before he released himself, rolled off and immediately started snoring.

She had hoped that he would pass out on top of her as he had so many times before. No such luck tonight.

Megan quietly got up and went to take a warm shower. Just touching herself made her cringe in pain. Megan could not remember the last time she was made love to; pleasurable love, where every touch is gentle and loving and caring and where your body is taken to the heights of passion with a release so strong, that you are almost on the brink of total madness. When she attempted to touch herself to get some kind of release, it was so painful that she couldn't even do it.

Megan dried off and quickly crawled back into bed. She drifted off to sleep on a tear soaked pillow.

She woke up to the sound of the phone ringing; it was her sister and best friend Michelle, "Hey sleepy head, let's go get a pedicure today".

Megan groggily said, "Sure, come get me around eleven". She glanced over to the other side of the bed; Bill was already gone.

She got up and got dressed, every inch of her body hurt, but she had to start her day as 'the great pretender'. First she had to start with some concealer, then her full-coverage make-up. She made sure that her bangs were perfect and the rest of her hair framed her face.

Next she had to remove the bandage from her wrist; she was going to have to be very careful with this hand today she thought. She quickly swallowed some extra-strength Advil, just as she heard the familiar honk of Michelle's car.

CHAPTER 2

Hiding The Truth

As Megan stepped out of her house that sunny morning, anyone who saw her would never have guessed that she was the victim of continuous and horrific domestic abuse. At five one she was very short, and was not fat by any means, but she was still a healthy one hundred and forty pounds.

Her red hair which was still its same natural hue, and had made her the most adorable five year old child, was made more attractive with high and low lights that complimented her complexion. She could never figure out how her sister and her brother were both over five feet nine, but yet she was so short. And even more strangely, they both had dark hair.

As she got into the car with Michelle, she hugged her sister and asked her how their mom was doing. Michelle responded by telling her that mom was doing fine and was looking forward to seeing her on Friday for dinner.

"How's Bill?" Michelle asked.
"He is doing great".

"How is his drinking Megan?"
"Ok Michelle, are we going to have a fun day or are we going to spend it talking about Bill's alleged drinking problem?"

A Michelle pulled out of the driveway, she glanced over at her sister, and couldn't help but wonder how many bruises were the oversized sunglasses and the heavy make-up hiding today; and she also couldn't help but notice that Megan's wrist appeared to be swollen.

Megan had long hidden the abuse. Now, she wished that she had listened to that little voice deep in her mind; the one with all the logical reservations. William was so handsome, that the first time she saw him she was determined to have him all to herself.

William was her brother Max's roommate in college, and would accompany him home on holidays and other breaks they got away from school. Megan remembered asking Max if William didn't have his own family to go home to.

He responded by telling her that William's mother was an alcoholic and his father was a no good wife beater, who more than once allowed his discipline of William to cross the line into abuse.

Needless to say, William enjoyed spending time with the Hullender family. They were stable, no one ever raised their voices, except in laughter and they genuinely loved and supported each other. How he wished that his own family was like that.

No wonder his sister went to live with their aunt in another state and never returned. Except for the occasional phone calls to their mother, no one ever heard from her.

William marveled at how his friend Max's family prayed before each meal and actually ate together, around the table. They played games together and even went to church every Sunday as a family.

Sure they had wine and vodka and other spirits in the house, but no one drank like it was the last day on earth, or some sort of race to the finish. They drank in moderation, at family gatherings or if someone stopped by unexpectedly around the holidays.

William thought to himself that alcohol did not survive very long at his house. His mother was once a beautiful woman, but after years of over consumption, coupled with the missing teeth (courtesy of his dad) and the broken jaw, she was not even a shadow of her former self.

He was named after his father, but he preferred to be called Bill, as not to confuse him with William senior.

One Spring Break holiday as William was again visiting with Max, Megan walked into her brother's room and saw them smoking what was definitely *not* Malboros. She was furious at her brother for going against everything their parents had taught them. She promised not to tell her mom or dad, if they promised not to disrespect her parents' house ever again.

William saw the passion and genuine concern in Megan's eyes and was touched by her caring, motherly nature.

"There goes the mother of my kids", he joked to Max. Max took one last long puff, coughed violently then responded, "man I think she likes you, you have my blessing, just don't fuck with my sister's heart or I will hunt you down man".

"She likes me? Why didn't you say something to me bro."
"Yea, she is always asking me questions about you".
"What kind of questions man?"
"Well" Max slowly drawled, "like if you have a girlfriend back at school, and if you date a lot of people, and if you were a nice guy; ya know the usual shit when a girl is interested".

"How come you never told me before man".

"You never asked"

After that it seemed like everything fell into place with Megan and William. They became the best of friends, staying up late reading Spider-Man comics together; William was an avid collector, and he trusted no one with his prized collection but Megan. They would spend hours next to each other reading, occasionally stopping to look up and smile at each other.

Mrs. Wells, William's long suffering mother grew to love Megan; she thought that Megan was good for her son. Megan noticed that each time she would visit, that Mrs. Wells was always seated at the table with a large bottle of vodka in front of her. She just sat at the kitchen table quietly drinking, never bothering to check on her son and Megan.

They always left the bedroom door open and they never disrespected her home. Mrs. Wells was just thankful that William was getting close to a nice girl from a seemingly normal family.

Megan, on the other hand, couldn't help but wonder what horrible turn this woman's life must have taken to cause her to hate herself so much.

One of Megan's favorite things to do was walk on the beach, and William indulged her. She didn't know if he liked it or not but he was always there to hold her hand. The two of them would sit for hours just staring at the water and talking; they talked about everything.

When William opened up to Megan about his family life and how he grew up, she was shocked and could not believe that he endured such a horrible family life. Part of her felt sorry for him, but the other part, was having doubts about their future together. Would he turn out to be like his father?

But William always stressed that he wanted to be nothing like his father, and that he would never lay a finger on a woman; not after he saw what his mother endured at the hands of her husband.

William promised Megan that once he graduated college, they would start their life together. However, nature had other plans for them; a year before William's graduation, Megan found herself late and rushing to the pharmacy to buy a pregnancy test.

She was afraid to tell William, but figured that she might as well, because they were going to be married anyway. When the two lines appeared, Megan started crying; not tears of joy, but tears of regret and shame. She would have to tell her parents and they would know that she had been secretly having sex.

To her surprise, her parents although disappointed and a bit upset, did not make a big deal out of it. Her mother said to her that since they were planning to get married anyway, to just speed up the wedding a bit.

CHAPTER 3

The End Of Innocence

William on the other hand was so furious that he slammed his hand into the wall so hard that he actually fractured his wrist. If there were never any signs before, that should have been the first big sign of William's temper.

When William saw Megan crying he immediately ran over to her to comfort her, not even stopping to tend to his now bruised and rapidly swelling wrist. Megan was starting to feel a deep feeling of discomfort and doubt, but realized that it was too late; she was pregnant and had to get married. Yes, she did love William but she could not shake the feeling of uneasiness and doom that seem to be lurking over and around her.

Even though Megan's parents wanted the big elaborate church wedding that most girls dream of, she had other ideas; Megan got *her* dream wedding.

There she was perched on top of the cliff by the old light house with only a crown of flowers serving as her wedding veil and an empire waist cream colored chiffon gown blowing in the evening wind.

The rushing sound of the waves hitting the rocks was all the music she needed. Michelle was of course her maid of honor, and to top it all off, Megan was barefooted; just as she had always imagined her wedding would be.

Only immediate family and a few close friends made up the almost twenty wedding guests. She kissed William as the sun set on the horizon and they became Mr. & Mrs. Wells; for better or for worse.

They did not immediately purchase a house, even though Mr. Hullender insisted that they accept his offer of a small two bedroom house as their starter home. William was adamant that he didn't want any handouts and flatly refused.

So they moved into a townhouse about fifteen miles from her parents' house. Since Megan was almost four months pregnant, they decided that she would not immediately look for a job but finish her last couple semesters of college and graduate with her Bachelor's in Business Management as planned.

Megan could not believe that even though her life had taken an unexpected turn, that things were actually falling into place. They would visit her parents on Sundays for dinner, and even though they did not have a lot of money, they would still manage to have lots of fun catching a matinee movie or the two for one special at the local restaurant.

William never seemed to want to visit his family though; Megan never pressured him because she knew his story and his reasons. Even though things seem fine and normal,

Megan could not shake the very uneasy feeling in the pit of her stomach. She was also having increased concerns with his drinking. She didn't think he had a problem, but she did think that he didn't need to drink so much.

In the evenings when he would return from his job at the insurance company he would have a beer to unwind; nothing wrong with that. But then that beer turned into a six pack, then a twelve pack, then a twelve pack with a few shots of vodka.

Megan tried to tell herself that William was going through a lot right now, being the breadwinner and all. Her mother and father secretly gave her money, but she dared not tell William; he would take it as an insult. So he was under the impression that she was a thrifty spender and really knew how to budget, because they never lacked anything, and the bills were always paid on time.

She began to feel like if she became the perfect wife then he would not drink so much and that she could provide him with the happy, stable home that he always dreamed of. But what Megan didn't realize or was too naïve to see was that William was slowly descending into the same bottomless, seemingly helpless pit that both his parents were already in.

If the house was a bit cleaner, if all the bills were paid on time, if I have sex with him when he wants, he will see that I truly love him and he will slow down on his drinking. Megan's thoughts ran away with her.

One evening while in her fifth month of pregnancy she was seated on the couch with her feet propped up watching Dr. Phil on the television, and the aroma of baked chicken coming from the kitchen, Megan got a call from her doctor's office.

They had called to confirm her appointment for the next day; they were going to find out the sex of the baby.

Unfortunately, William couldn't go with her, he could not afford to take off work. So her mom and her sister were more than happy to fill in for him; they figured they could make a girl's afternoon of it and have lunch and maybe fit a pedicure in.

CHAPTER 4

Twice As Nice

As she relaxed on the table and the doctor put the lukewarm ultrasound gel on her growing belly, she was secretly wishing that William was there to share the moment with her. Sure she loved that her mom and sister were there, but is was not the same as having her husband, the father of her child there by her side to hold her hand.

Her mother being a retired nurse got a look of surprise and utter joy on her face all of a sudden. She was the only one that was really paying attention to the ultrasound screen. Megan asked her mom what the matter was; all her mother could do was lean down with tears in her eyes and kiss her on the forehead.

The doctor finally spoke, "well Mrs. Wells, it seems like your mother already figured it out, but it looks like you are having twins".

If Megan wasn't already flat on her back she would have fallen down.

"What?" she exclaimed.

"He said twins Megan, twins, can you believe it?" Michelle chimed in, with a huge grin on her face.

"But how....what happ....how could?" Megan was stuttering out partial questions.

"Megan, I was a twin, but my sister died at birth, and my father, your grandfather was a twin also".

"Well now is a fine time to tell me the family history mom, don't you think?"

Megan was happy, scared, surprised and a whole lot of other feelings that she could not describe, all rolled into one. What she did know for sure was that she couldn't wait to tell William. Her mother was already dialing her cell phone to tell her husband that he was going to be the grandfather of twins.

The doctor was slowly moving the ultrasound instrument over her belly, gently pressing in and taking pictures when he suddenly exclaimed,

"Gotcha; one of them is definitely a boy, no mistake, I cannot get the second one to open the legs, but being that shy, I would bet anything that it is a girl".

"A boy *and* a girl" Megan could not hold back her tears any longer. Now both Michelle and her mom were crying so hard that the doctor had no choice but to laugh.

"Well Mrs. Wells, regardless of the sex of the other twin, they are surely going to have a lot of love".

"Thanks doctor" Megan whispered, still in shock.

Megan had a wonderful lunch with her mom and sister, they had lots to celebrate and celebrate they did. She enjoyed a virgin pina colada, while her mother and Michelle both enjoyed a glass of wine.

"No wonder I am getting so big so fast" Megan told them. "I cannot believe that I am having twins".

She couldn't wait to tell William, she just knew how thrilled he would be to have a son, maybe even two sons.

"So how do you think William will take the news of having twins?" Michelle asked, "you know how proud he is about taking anything, and you are going to need a lot of help, especially financially".

Megan didn't tell them, but the minute she found out that she was having twins, as excited and shocked as she was, she was also feeling a bit nervous. She couldn't help but wonder what William's reaction might be. But instead she responded by saying that William was not as bad as they made him out to be, that he just happens to be fiercely independent. Michelle and her mom both exchanged knowing glances as an indication to leave it alone because they knew that Megan was going to defend William all the way.

When Megan got home, she prepared a nice dinner for her husband; she had stopped at the liquor store and bought a cheap bottle of champagne for him and a bottle of sparkling apple cider for herself. Tonight was going to be a celebration of love, hope, new beginnings, new life......

Later that evening William walked through the door to find Megan smiling lovingly at him; he wondered what was there to smile about. She ran into his arms and hugged him, but all he wanted a beer.

She told him to sit down, he reluctantly did and she broke the news to him. William was silent for a moment, he then got up and slowly walked toward her. Megan held her arms open expecting a loving embrace, instead he grabbed her by the throat and pushed her up against the wall.

CHAPTER 5

The Monster Exposed

"What the hell are you saying Megan, twins, for God sake I can barely feed the two of us, you sit around all day long on your fat ass and eat every goddamn thing in the fridge, then you tell me that I am going to have two more mouths to feed?"

At this point Megan was beyond shocked, she could hardly breathe, but he continued to choke her. Megan smelled his breath and realized that he had started drinking before reaching home.

Megan tried to stammer out a response but she was slowly starting to lose consciousness; just as she was about to pass out and everything was starting to go black before her eyes he let go and let her body slump to the floor.

Megan slowly got to her knees and tried to get up; she was so scared and hurt at that moment that she could not find the words to say. She had just used one leg to raise herself up when William came at her again, this time kicking her with the force of a wild mule in the middle of her belly.

Megan was now so scared that she started to panic, she just knew that he was going to kill her. She started to scream in pain, something wasn't right, her stomach was cramping with such force that she cried out in agony.

She heard herself screaming, "William, William, what are you doing, please stop, please do not hurt my babies, please William stop, help, help!" There was no way that she could reach the phone, she could barely move, she was hoping that a neighbor would hear her cries and call the police.

Through her pleadings and pain, William continue to kick her with his boots which by now were no longer an item of clothing, but a weapon.

Megan started vomiting uncontrollably and she realized that she had started to bleed. "Oh my god, I am going to lose my babies!"

William was in such a state of frenzy that he didn't even notice that Megan had passed out. When he looked down and saw that the woman that he loved was covered in blood and two of her teeth were on the floor next to her, he couldn't believe his eyes. He quickly dialed 911 and rushed to her side.

He held her head in his lap as the tears flowed down his cheeks, "what have I done, what have I done?" he lamented.

Then he realized that he could be in a whole heap of trouble, he had to think fast. He glanced around the room; he then jumped up and quickly lifted Megan up and set her at the bottom of the stairs. He then pulled the coffee table over the spot where she had been.

He picked up the teeth and placed them a few inches from her body and just as he heard the sirens in the distance, he looked up to the heavens and said, "God, please forgive me, I do not want to be like my father".

When Megan woke up in the hospital, she could not figure out what had happened, or why her mother, brother, sister and William were all sitting around either sniffing or noticeably crying.

She had and IV in her arm, an oxygen mass was coverd her face. Megan made a light grunt, and realized that she was in the worst pain ever; she did not think that pain of this magnitude was possible.

"She's awake" whispered Michelle, "Oh my God, what should we tell her; for heaven's sake *should* we tell her?"

Michelle rang for the nurse, who was there in the room in less than 30 seconds flat. When she came in and saw that Megan was awake, she walked over to her and felt her pulse, and took her temperature.

Megan realized that one of left arm was in a cast, but the worst thing that she discovered was that in place of her beautiful baby bump, she now had a somewhat flat stomach which hurt like hell.

She was too groggy and too drugged up to figure anything out, so she slowly lifted the mask off of her face and asked the nurse, "where are my babies, did I have the babies?"

The nurse patted her shoulder, and said "now, now just try to get some rest, the doctor will be in to see you shortly". She then gave the family members a very sympathetic and nervous smile and quickly left the room.

Mrs. Hullender was the first to go to her bedside.

"Megan, we love you very much, can you tell us what happened?"

Before Megan could even form her words, William said, "didn't I tell you that she slipped and fell down the stairs, why are you asking her this?"

Megan's father got up and walked over to William, "don't you raise your voice at my wife, she can ask her anything she chooses to; things do not add up and you damn well know it, we need some answers, I want to know why I no longer have my grandbabies!"

Mr. Hullender had blurted out the last line without thinking. Megan, at this point, still did not know what had happened. When Megan heard that, she tried to get up, but the pain was immeasurable, "what do you mean, you no longer have your grandbabies daddy, where are they?"

Michelle rushed to Megan's other side, it was now or never.

"Megan, we have some very bad news for you, we did not want you to find out like this. Oh Megan, I am so sorry".

By now everyone was crying loudly, including Megan, she was partially crying because she was in so much pain, but she felt that her tears were for something else; something much worse. Her room was filled with flowers, and as she glanced at the closest arrangement, she barely made out the phrase, "*Our Condolences*". She did not want to hear what Michelle was about to say,

"Megan, the babies died, oh my God mom I cannot do this!"

Mrs. Hullender asked Megan again if she remembered what happened and what *did* happen. Megan's eyes shot over to William who was sitting with his head in his hands with tears flowing though his fingers. He looked up at her, and the pain she saw in his eyes seemed equal to the physical pain she was now feeling. She could not and would not allow her husband to go to jail. She closed her eyes, breathed heavily and said,

"Mom, I think I remember falling down the stairs".

"Are my babies really gone?"

"Yes, my dear, we are going to arrange services once you are well enough to leave the hospital" said Mrs. Hullender through her tears.

"I knew I had a son, I had already named him Jacob, what was the other?"

"A girl" was the feeble reply from her mother. Amidst tears, Megan slowly said, "Natalie", and immediately fell back to sleep.

All the while Max was seated over by the window, silently mourning his family's loss. He didn't have any solid proof, but he knew that something was wrong with this picture. It just did not add up, his sister didn't just fall, she looked as though she was hit by a tractor trailer.

The nurse popped her head back in the room and whispered, "I think you should leave her to get some rest, did you tell her?"
"Yes, we did", said Michelle.
"But did you tell her *everything*?"

CHAPTER 6

Painful Reality

As Megan and Michelle were eating lunch, Michelle casually said to her,

"Megan, I was thinking that maybe we could go on a little cruise together; ya know, just us girls and have some fun".

"I do not think I can, but thanks for trying, really I am fine; Michelle, please don't tell mom, but I was thinking of adopting a baby".

"WHAT, are you crazy, you would bring a child into that home?"

"What is wrong with my home?"

"Megan, I know that we have been treating you with kid gloves ever since your ordeal, but let me be frank with you. I am sick and tired of William treating you like his own personal punching bag. He treats you like shit, he beats you up".

"No he does not, and keep your voice down" Megan interrupted.

"Megan, no one is stupid but you; I know, mom knows, dad knows, Max knows, the neighbors know, your friends know, hell even the dog knows. And take those damn shades off at the table, I know you have a black eye".

By now Megan had burst into tears,

"Michelle, why are you doing this, now is not the time".

"If not now when, huh, when you are six feet under?"

Megan got up to leave when Michelle grabbed her by the wrist to sit back down;

Megan winced in pain.

"See what I mean, now tell me how you fell or slammed it in the car door by mistake, go on Megan, what story are you going to come up with this time?"

Michelle felt desperate, she had to talk to some sense into her only sister, otherwise she was going to end up dead way before her time. Michelle knew that as much as she wanted Megan away from that monster, that she had to go about it a different way.

She just couldn't understand how a beautiful, intelligent woman from a good, stable family could end up in an abusive relationship and on top of that defend the bastard; the man who murdered his own two children. What was it going to take to get Megan to see the light?

Megan sat back down, but could not finish her salad; instead, over a glass of merlot, she remembered the day she returned from the hospital after loosing her babies.

She wiped a tear from under her shades as she remembered before leaving the hospital, the doctor had reluctantly told her that the bandage was from where they had to do an emergency C-section in order to save her life, and unfortunately an emergency hysterectomy as well.

Losing the babies was hell in itself, but finding out that she could never, ever give birth was like being given a death sentence to the gallows.

Sure she went to counseling at the urge of all the family members, but she just did not see the purpose of it. She had a medicine cabinet full of 'feel-good, make me numb and turn me into a zombie' pills, all strong enough to disable an elephant.

Effexor, Seroquel, Wellbutrin, were just some of the many prescriptions she took every night. Prayers and medication, medication and prayers. It seemed like a never ending cycle, and she was not really getting anywhere emotionally. Hell, she was not even honest with her counselor; she defended William every chance she got and never admitted any type of wrong doing on his part.

She always told the counselor and her family that William was a great husband and a great provider and that he truly loved her.

Somewhere deep down within her, she knew that she was lying, but what could she do? She did not want to end her marriage. It became very awkward, she prayed for God to stop the abuse, and she honestly did everything in her power to prevent it.

She was a very good wife, she kept the house spotless, she cooked, she ironed, she waited on her husband hand and foot. She did everything that she thought would stop him; except for one thing, she did not leave.

Whenever she would call William's mom to get some type of sympathy, the elder Mrs. Wells would laugh at her and tell her,

"Girl you knew what you were getting into, but you thought you were too good for this to happen to you. So either, you are going to come to my funeral or I will be at yours. He is just like his father; so let me deal with mine, and you deal with yours, I cannot help you".

Megan would always think to herself, how dare Mrs.Wells compare herself to her. Their situations are totally different. But each time a foot connected with her ribcage or each time she was all black and blue, she would quietly wonder, "are our situations really different?"

After the babies died, William backed off for a while. He seemed genuinely remorseful and saddened by his actions. He waited on Megan hand and foot, he even slowed down his drinking for a few months. He didn't stop completely though, he just slowed down, meaning instead of an entire bottle of Vodka, he would only drink about half.

He was the perfect husband for a while (perfect by Megan's definition). They even brought themselves to partially discuss what happened the evening she lost the babies, but they stopped short and vowed never to talk about it, ever.

William on the other hand, was secretly afraid that at any moment, she was going to lose it and scream to the world exactly what did happen. She might as well have done that, because her family all hated him; Max and him were no longer friends and he was not welcomed at the Hullender house any longer.

Megan had no friends other than her sister, and her counselor. She lost quite a few good girlfriends because, each time one of them confided in her that William had touched them inappropriately or said something to them that he clearly shouldn't have, she would always throw them out and accuse them of lying on her husband and trying to break up her marriage.

So after many years of this, Megan was left with no friends at all; and for her it was ok because she was always tired of them giving her advice that she never solicited from them in the first place.

She remembered one instance with her good friend Camille. They had known each other all through high school and had become like sisters. They shared everything, right down to lip gloss.

Camille was one of only a few friends at her wedding. They had always made a promise to each other that they would be godmother to each other's children one day. A pact was also made that no matter what, they would never allow anyone, especially a man, to come in between their friendship.

So when Camille called her crying early one Sunday morning and asked if they could meet immediately, Megan thought that maybe she had boyfriend trouble or something and just needed a shoulder to cry on.

To Megan's surprise, Camille was so distraught that she could hardly speak. Camille started out by giving Megan a huge hug. She said that she was at home reading when William called her and told her that he needed to secretly meet with her and talk about planning a surprise birthday party for Megan.

She anxiously agreed and didn't think anything of it. So she told him to stop by after work with his ideas and a date for the party and they would compare notes and get the guest list started.

She paused to blow her nose, she then continued, "Megan, I am so sorry".

She told Megan that by the time William arrived, her parents were gone to catch a movie, so she was home alone. She said that she noticed alcohol on William's breath, but didn't think anything of it, she just figured that he had a couple after work beers with the guys.

She said that they sat down and she started telling him what she came up with and how excited she was and couldn't wait to see the look on Megan's face when she found out.

All of a sudden William had gotten up from the chair he was sitting in and went and sat next to her on the couch. She told Megan that at first she wasn't uncomfortable, but did notice the potency of the alcohol on his breath from so close.

All of a sudden he started to rub her thigh and she jumped up and asked him what he thought that he was doing. He responded by grabbing her arm and pulling her back down on the couch.

Camille went on to say that that was when she started to become afraid because the look in his eyes was pure evil. She said by then he had cupped one of her breast in his hand and proceeded to rip her blouse open.

By now Camille was crying even harder. She told Megan that she managed to get away from him and run to the kitchen where her father kept a small 22 caliber handgun.

Camille said that she turned around and pointed it directly at William and told him to get the hell out of her house or she was going to call the police. Camille recounted that when he saw the gun, he backed off and begged her not to tell Megan, then he laughed and added, "go ahead bitch, tell her, she would never believe you".

Camille got up and went over to hug Megan again, when to her shock and dismay, Megan jumped up and screamed at her,

"You fucking liar, how dare you say those things about my husband?"

Camille was so flabbergasted that she was rendered speechless, her only response was,

“Megan, this is me we are talking about, me, your best friend”.

“Best friend? You are not a friend, you could never be a friend to any woman; you throw yourself at my husband and when he rejects you, you accuse him of coming on to you; what is it Camille, huh? Is it jealousy, you couldn’t stand the fact that I got married and you are still single and living at home with your parents. You are not my friend, and I never want to see or hear from you ever again! Camille, you are now dead to me”.

Camille could not hold back any longer, yes she was hurt, very hurt, but now she had become very angry.

“Megan if this is the way you want it, so be it, you do not have to believe me; but I have never betrayed our friendship, ever, and you just broke my heart and my trust, if you never want to see me again, so be it. But mark my words, Megan I will be coming to your funeral real soon. Have a good fucking life, or should I say death?”

As Megan and Michelle tried to get through what turned out to be a very awkward lunch. Michelle again asked Megan if she would at least think about going on the cruise with her.

Megan promised that she would think about it and ask William. Michelle was about to inquire as to why she had to ask the bastard’s permission, but decided against it.

She did not want to upset Megan anymore. But she did have one last question,

"Megan, have you at least tried to talk to Camille at all?"

CHAPTER 7

The Devil Lives With Me

When Michelle dropped Megan off at home, she pleaded with her one last time. "Megan, please move back home with us, or if you think that he will not leave you alone, we can send you out of state, but Megan please, please get away from him. You are not even the same sister I remember."

Megan looked at her sister's sad face and replied,

"Oh Michelle you have a wild imagination, how many times do I have to tell you all that I am fine, yes William and I have our problems like every other couple, but there is nothing going on out of the ordinary. Now go on and tell mom I love her and I will call her later."

Michelle pulled off with tears in her eyes, and her heart aching.

Megan went into the house and sat down, everything from over the past few years flooded into her head, and suddenly she felt overwhelmed. She was also getting a bit scared, because she had to hurry and make dinner for William, he would be home in a few short hours. She baked some pork chops and roasted some red potatoes along with some green beans.

When she got through she took a quick shower and reapplied her make-up; she had to look perfect for William. Then she started to become afraid again, she knew what was going to happen when he got home. If she breathed too loudly she was going to hit her.

She started to panic, and she picked up the phone to call Michelle to come over and get her, then she hung it up without dialing the number. She then told herself that she needed to call Camille and apologize and beg for her forgiveness, but she decided against it. Camille would never forgive her, not after the way she treated her.

She started to pace back and forth frantically, what was she going to do, she thought, how could she avoid a beating tonight.

Then she had an idea, if she was knocked out he couldn't beat her and even of he tried to have his way with her she would be totally unconscious.

Megan rushed up to her bathroom and got all her pill bottles, all the ones that had warnings like, "may cause drowsiness' and 'do not operate a motor vehicle….' She opened all of them and poured almost half from each bottle into her hand and went to the kitchen and grabbed a beer.

She stood at the sink with tears in her eyes, and looked up and prayed, "God I am not doing what you think I am doing, I just want to go to sleep, I cannot take it tonight lord, I just can't;

please just let me fall asleep and wake up in the morning once he is already gone".

Megan swallowed a cocktail of almost fourteen very powerful antidepressant and antipsychotic pills with a couple swigs of beer. She sat on the couch shaking in fear; her subconscious knew what she was doing, but as with everything else in her life she was even in denial about trying to kill herself.

When she started to feel lethargic and could barely move with her eyesight blurred Megan got really scared and picked up the phone, she hit the one number that speed dialed Michelle's cell phone.

Meanwhile Michelle was at the table eating dinner with their parents when her cell phone started to ring. Her father was a bit upset at the intrusion during dinner, but when Michelle announced that it was Megan, his face change into a smile.

"Hello" Michelle said, "Hello, Megan?" the only thing that Michelle could hear was a drawled "haaallllo, Mich….". Michelle kept shouting for Megan to answer her and asking if everything was alright, the phone line went dead.

Michelle jumped up and said to her parents, "I think something is wrong with Megan, call 911 and send them over there, I am on my way".

Mr. Hullender quickly dialed 911 and gave them the street address to Megan's house while Michelle jumped into her car and sped off. All the while she tried dialing Megan's number, but the home number was busy and there was no answer on Megan's cell.

The only thing that Michelle could think of was that William had finally done it, he had killed her sister. Michelle drove as fast as traffic allowed with tears flowing down her cheeks.

Not too far behind her were her parents, as soon as 911 was dispatched to Megan's house, Mr. Hullender had grabbed his wife's hand and his shot gun and was out the door. He was prepared to spend the rest of his life in prison, because if William had murdered his daughter, by God almighty he was going to put a few bullets into his skull.

Michelle pulled up just as paramedics were frantically working to revive her sister. She was crying hysterically and trying to get to Megan's seemingly lifeless body. A police officer held her back and told her to please allow the paramedics to do their job.

She could see Megan's face, it was a pale blue and was very still. They heard a paramedic shout, "let's get her to the hospital now, I think we are losing her".

They rushed past Michelle and into the waiting ambulance and sped away. Mr. Hullender pulled up and before he could get out of the car, Michelle jumped in and told him to follow the ambulance to the hospital.

Megan's parents kept asking what had happened, but Michelle had no idea, she told them that William was no where to be found and that it didn't seem like he had anything to do with what had happened.

They arrived at the hospital, but there was no word on Megan's condition; no one was saying anything. Michelle called Camille to ask her if she had spoken to Megan and if she knew what was going on with her.

Camille was clearly upset but informed Michelle that she hadn't spoken with Megan for a while. Now Michelle was really confused. A lot seem to be going on in Megan's life that she was not aware of. Nevertheless she told Camille that they were praying really hard but it didn't look good for Megan.

Camille got off the phone with tears in her eyes and rushed to the hospital. She thought to herself, Megan might not be a friend to me, but I have always been a friend to her and I do not want anything to happen to her.

Back at the hospital Megan's parents and sister were praying out loud asking God to please spare Megan's life. After what seemed like an eternity, the doctor walked out and introduced himself.

He reassured them that Megan was alive, and that it was a miracle that she was. Michelle, her parents and Camille all cried out with relief and thanks. The doctor continued by asking if Megan was depressed and if she had ever tried to harm herself before. They all looked at each other, and nodded to Michelle. Michelle told the doctor that yes her sister was seeing a therapist and was on medication for depression.

The doctor then asked if anything life changing happened recently. They all looked at each other for a moment, then Mrs. Hullender blurted out, "her husband beats her".

The doctor said, "Well she ingested enough pills to kill a horse, lucky for her we pumped her stomach and as able to save her life, five or ten more minutes without medical attention she would have been dead".

"Can we see her now?"
"No not right now, she is in a medically induced coma and we still have to monitor her closely, she is being moved to ICU".

Michelle urged her parents to go home and get some rest, and told them that she would stay at the hospital no matter how long it took for Megan to wake up. Camille said that she would stay as well.

As they waited, Michelle and Camille started talking. It was then that they compared stories and were now one hundred percent sure that Megan was an abused and brainwashed woman. Camille told Michelle what had happened, as shocked as Michelle was over what William did; she was even more shocked and surprised when she learned of Megan's reaction.

She could not believe how Megan treated Camille.

"This certainly does not sound like Megan, she loves you Camille, you are her best friend in the entire world; hell I was even a bit jealous of your friendship with her, because she always seemed to be closer to you".

Camille shook her head and said to Michelle,

"Ya know, at first I was angry, but then I started to do some research on abused women and realized that Megan fits every single description, so even though I kept my distance, I forgave her and I pray for her every day; and I really, really miss her.

It is like Megan died a long time ago and was replaced by a zombie, she is not herself".

Michelle agreed.

William got home to a house with the door kicked in and neighbors standing outside. He learned from one of them that his wife had been rushed to the hospital. He hurried and got into his car and drove as fast as he could.......to the nearest bar.

When Megan came to, she looked around the hospital room and saw that she was all alone. What had happened? She feebly reached for the call button and pushed it. It took a while, but a nurse came in with a doctor not far behind.

The nurse did not look friendly at all, and the doctor seemed pretty cold as well. They both looked at her and announced that they had called for her sister to be there so that they could tell her what was happening.

To Megan's surprise, when Michelle walked into the room Camille was with her. At the sight of Camille, all Megan could do was sob uncontrollably.

They both rushed over to her and held her hands crying. Between sobs, Michelle said,
"Megan, we came so close to losing you".

The doctor interrupted by saying,

"Under the circumstances, and the fact that this was clearly a suicide attempt, we are going to have you transferred to a

Psychiatric Hospital for further evaluation; of course we will not move you until you are medically stable".

"Suicide attempt?" Megan's eyes widened.
"I did not try to commit suicide".

"Mrs. Wells, call it what you wish, but this was a suicide attempt if I ever saw one, and I have seen quite a few in my time".

"No doctor, I was not trying to kill myself, I was just, I was just….." Megan's voice trailed off.

Michelle whispered to the doctor, "is she so deep in denial that she is actually denying trying to kill herself?"

"Yes, if she convinces herself that she was just trying to get some sleep, then what happened in her life and her trying to end it all would not be real; Psychiatry isn't my area of medicine, that is why I am going to transfer her so that she gets the help that she so desperately needs".

"But I do not want to go, I want to go home".

"I am afraid that you do not have a say in the matter Mrs. Wells, once we determined that you are now a danger to yourself and maybe to others, we have no choice but to send you for a full psychological evaluation".

"Michelle, please do not let them do this to me, you know I am not crazy" Megan pleaded.

"Megan, please do not make this difficult, you need this; we all know you need this. Please, please do this, at least for mom and dad, they are so worried about you".

"But Michelle, please do not let them do this".

"It is out of my hands Megan; you really do need this".

The doctor then announced that they had to leave, but he reassured them that Megan would be closely monitored. Michelle and Camille both leaned down to kiss Megan goodbye. Megan looked up at Camille with tears in her eyes and whispered, "I am sorry". Camille hugged her and said, "I love you Megan".

Back at the house, William had already polished off a bottle of whisky. When he got back home and saw that Megan still wasn't there, he had asked his neighbor to help him fix the front door. Then he drank some more.

Mr. Hullender had already made his mind up that even though William was no where around when Megan had her "unfortunate accident" that he was still somehow behind this entire thing. Mr. Hullender voiced his concerns to his wife, who was sitting with her head in her hands.

Mrs. Hullender looked up at her husband and said, "we all know that, tell me something that I do not already know".

"I want to kill him", Mr. Hullender responded.

"What did you say, Pete?"

"I said I want the bastard dead".

"Pete, you cannot go around saying things like that"

"Well, it is either him or Megan; which one do you want to see dead?"

"You do not know what you are saying Pete, you do not know what you are saying". Mrs. Hullender buried her face in her hands and cried.

CHAPTER 8

Dear God Please...

Back at the hospital, Megan was drifting in and out of consciousness. Even though her thoughts were racing, she couldn't really concentrate and focus those thoughts. She did not admit to attempting suicide and did not want to believe it.

Her feelings were all a big mess; she wanted to go to sleep and not wake up, but yet when she saw the pain on her family's face she wanted to be here for them.

She tried her best to remember exactly what happened; she remembered having lunch with Michelle and then Michelle drove her back home. Then she remembered this overwhelming fear and then she was in the hospital. What had happened? Did Bill hurt her again? She could not gather her thoughts.

What she did figure out was that something was wrong; very, very wrong. From what she remembered from the conversation, they were going to send her to a Mental hospital. Am I really crazy? Did I suffer a breakdown?

As she slowly opened her eyes, she looked up and prayed for the first time in a very long time,

"Dear Lord Jesus, what ever is happening to me, I have allowed it to go on for too long. Please, please I need you now more than ever."

Tears were flowing onto the pillow now. Megan had shed tears on pillows quite a bit, but this time it was different.

She continued,

"I have made a lot of mistakes and caused my family and the people I love the most a lot of pain and heartache. I have lied over and over again, please dear heavenly father forgive me for all I have done. I am at my absolute weakest right now, and I need you now more than ever.

Please, please, please give me the strength to do what I need to do to survive. I am alive for a reason Lord, please give me the strength to fulfill that reason. I thank you for life, and I am sorry that I took it for granted all of this time. Heavenly father I am now asking you for strength; strength that I never had. Please Lord, help me, please help me, help me, help me, hel……".

Megan drifted back off to sleep.

CHAPTER 9

Vengeance Belongs To God

Michelle was angry, hurt, revengeful, and just plain sick to her stomach. She wanted William dead; dead, dead, dead!!! 'That bastard', she thought out loud. She began to plan what she was going to do and how she was going to do it.

It had to be done before Megan's release to go home. Michelle sat on the edge of her bed thinking and wondering how she could go about having William killed and not be involved in it at all.

After a few moments, she held her head in her hands and said out loud,

"Oh my God, what am I thinking? I learned a long time ago to turn all my problems over to you, now I am trying to handle this myself, when I should be worrying about Megan and just getting her away from that monster".

Michelle pulled herself together and decided to run out to the store to get Megan some essentials, because she was most definitely NOT going over to the house to get anything. She was afraid to get into an altercation with William and for fear of what she might do to him. She was that angry.

Four days later Megan was discharged from the hospital directly into the care of the local Psychiatric facility. When she walked in she couldn't help but think that she did not belong in a place like this.

They dictated what time she woke up, what scheduled meetings she had to attend, what time to bathe, when and for how long she could use the phone and to top it all off she was sharing a room with a total stranger. Suppose this new roommate is a homicidal maniac? *What could be worse than this*? she asked herself.

Then as if a light bulb had gone off in her head, she said out loud,

"Being at home with Bill right now; that is what could be worse than this".

Her new roommate Ramona seemed sane enough; she was a young mother who had lost her job, no child support, no money. Apparently she had attempted suicide because life became too overwhelming and too much to bear. She asked Megan what she doing in a mental hospital.

"I took too many pills and they thought that I tried to commit suicide", Megan replied.

"Well you did try to, didn't you?"

"No, I did not try to kill myself"

"That is what we all say girlfriend, but deep down inside we know the truth"

"For the last time, I did NOT try to kill myself!" Megan screamed

"Oh well, you are not fooling anyone but yourself; it is called D-E-N-I-A-L, look it up"

Megan was so pissed that she wanted to punch Ramona out right there and then, but this little voice inside her told her not to. Everyone on her floor had to line up to get their medication from the nurse. None of the patients were allowed to have any type of medication on their person, at all, not even a damn Tylenol.

This entire setting was a completely new experience for Megan. She felt like she was in grade school all over again. She took her prescribed pills and went and sat at the table where a man was seated working on what seemed like a five thousand piece.

She tried to strike up a conversation, but he simply ignored her. She got up and went to her room. She was bored and the medication was starting to take effect, so she put on her pajamas and went to bed.

As she drifted off to sleep staring at the ceiling, she realized one thing. This was one of the most peaceful nights that she could remember in a very long time.

Wake up time was 5:45am, with shower to follow, then breakfast. Then it was individual counseling time. Megan actually felt rested, even though she had to wake up at that god forsaken hour.

She met with the resident Psychiatrist who was already seated and waiting for her.

"Nice to meet you, I am Dr. Reed; can I call you Megan?"

"Yes, nice to meet you too Dr. Reed"

"I see that you attempted suicide; tell me what was going through your mind at the moment and what got you to that point"

"Dr. Reed, I did not attempt suicide"

"I would say taking almost fifteen different pills is a sure fire way to end it all"

"But I didn't, I wasn't; I was just trying to get some sleep"

"Alright Megan, tell me about your home life; I understand that you are married, what is your husband like?"

Megan's thoughts began to race and so did her heart. What was she going to say? She held her head down trying to find the right words to say.

Dr. Reed had an idea of what Megan was going to say. She had sat across from Megan's type hundreds of time; quiet, shy, a bit jumpy, never quite making eye contact, wearing long sleeve and high collard clothing even though it was 90 degrees outside. Before allowing Megan a chance to open her mouth and lie, Dr. Reed addressed her,

"Megan, let me say this to you before you think for too long and make up some sorry story about how nobody understands your husband like you do, and that he had a very rough childhood , or that he was abused and he just needs time, and you are being patient with him because you do not want to abandon him, and that you know that deep down he truly loves you……Save it, I have heard it a million times. What I want to hear from you is how much longer you intend to live, what steps you are going to make to get away from this so call husband of yours, and if you do intend to live much longer, what you intend to do with that life".

Megan flew into a rage, "How dare you? You don't even know me or know anything about my life!!!"

She continued,

"I am sitting here vulnerable and depressed and yes, quite broken right now; I am here simply because the hospital said that I needed to be here. There is nothing wrong with me that medication cannot fix".

"Megan, you can fool your family, your friends and be in denial all you want, but be rest assured that you cannot fool me".

"Dr. Reed, I am fine, really"

"Ok, let's say for argument's sake that you are ok, why did you try to kill yourself, and why are there old bruises all over your body"

Silence –

"Megan, now that you know what to expect, can we continue? Remember, these sessions are going to be honest and upfront. I do not want you making any excuses or lie to me about anything. I cannot even begin to help you unless you are honest with yourself first".

Megan got up and went back to her room. Dr. Reed shook her head, she knew Megan's type all too well, she was just glad that she was alive and in a safe place now. She knew that in time Megan would open up; they always do.

Back in her room, Megan did not want to have another confrontation with Ramona. She was just another total stranger pretending to know all about her and her life.

Part of Megan wanted to go home and talk to Bill and convince him to start over and try to make their marriage work. She imagined that she could convince him to promise her that he wouldn't drink again or he wouldn't ever hit her again. She just knew that he would keep his promise; she just had to remind him how much she loved him.

The other part wanted to run away as far as she could for as long as she could. She was tired of so much pain.

Ramona interrupted her thoughts, "Hello, don't you have a session with Dr. Reed now?"

"Yes"
"Well aren't you late?"
"No, I just left early"
"What?"
"Didn't you hear me, I said I left early"
"Why?"
"It just wasn't for me ok; she didn't make any sense"
"Or is it that she just didn't buy into any of your denial and excuses bullshit?" Ramona quipped.

"Ok, Ramona, that is your name right? Well get this Ramona, I am not here because I need to be here, I am here because a mistake was made; I am not like you or the rest of the people here. So don't sit here and pretend like you know me or what I need". Megan was actually fuming.

"Well, I hope for your sake that you are right; but let me tell you one thing Megan, this is real life, and we only have one life; and when we spend it covering up other people's mistakes, and condoning other people's behavior and lying for other people and whatever the hell else you are doing, we are not really living at all.

Megan, I spent the majority of my life existing, not really living, but just existing from day to day. Almost every bone in my body has been broken, broken by a man who convinced me for years that it was my fault.

A man who each time he slammed my head against a wall told me that I made him do it. I lost my children to the state because I lied and covered up for him when he was accused of physically abusing them. I went through hell, so excuse me 'Miss. High and Mighty, I am too good for something like that to ever happen to me', you cannot fool me. I been there, done that and got a t-shirt to prove it".

"I-I-I didn't..." Megan stammered.

"Of course you wouldn't, it burns me up when I see women like you now; you walk around in pain, both physically and mentally, you are just shells of your former selves, you live to protect these bastards who do nothing but take your lives away in one form or another. If you are not walking around dead, you are literally dead".

"Well, if you are so perfect and you know everything, what the hell are you doing in here?"

"For your information, I found the courage to leave my 'bastard' over a year ago, but I somehow had a more difficult time leaving the alcohol. For so long, it was my crutch to dealing with everything, so when I finally got away from him, it came with me. I thought that I could handle it, and like everything else I was in denial for a long time. So here I am, after an overdose, making an attempt to get over another addiction in my life. Look, I didn't mean to come across so harsh, it just hurts me to the core to see 'me' all over again".

By now Megan was crying. She cried like she never cried before. Ramona walked over to Megan and sat next to her on one of the small twin sized beds in their room. She put her arms around her, and didn't say another word.

CHAPTER 10

Easier Said Than Done

Michelle answered her phone and was surprised to hear Megan's voice on the other end. She was also very happy to hear from her. She hadn't seen her in over a week; even when she dropped off some supplies for Megan, she didn't get to see her.

Michelle asked her how everything was going, and was surprised, shocked rather to hear Megan answer by asking her if she and their dad could go to her house and pack her things up.

"Are you kidding me Megan?"

"No Michelle, I am not, please go to the house after 7:30 in the morning and pack my stuff up and take it back to mom and dad's. I don't care about furniture or things like that, just my clothes and cosmetics and my pictures and keepsakes. Don't ask me anything right now, just please do me this favor. Please tell mom and dad that I love them very much and I will call them back really soon."

"Was that Megan on the phone, why didn't you let me talk to her?" Mrs. Hullender asked.
"Mom, you will not believe this, Megan is finally leaving William".
"What?"

"Yes, she didn't even ask about him; I was about to tell her that he keeps calling trying to find out where she is, but she didn't give me a chance to. Mom she didn't even sound like the Megan I know, she sounded confident and sure of herself; she told me exactly what she needed me to do".

"Wow is all I can say; let me go tell your father".

"Mom, tell him that I am renting a small U-haul truck, and first thing in the morning we are going to get her stuff from over there".

Megan was sure of one thing; she had to get away from William. It was as if a bell suddenly went off. Yes, she loved him, but he had become this stranger, this monster who stole all her dreams away, and who kept killing her spirit.

She knew that she was slowly dying when she actually could see herself in a casket. She saw her parents, her sister, brother, her friends, everyone she knew just standing over her grave crying and shaking their heads; all wondering if there was something they could have done to save her.

She did not want her very vivid hallucination to become a reality. But where could she start? She had set the ball rolling with a call to Michelle about helping her move. Megan was well aware that she had to be careful with this situation. No way no how could she agitate William.

The Psychiatrist told Megan that she could be released from inpatient care in a couple of days, but she had to come to outpatient care every day from 9a.m to 4p.m. She was also told that she had to continue her medications, and that a few more would be added upon her release.

On her last night at the facility, Megan sat up in bed thinking about her life, and trying to figure out where her life had taken that wrong turn. She was trying to remember the exact moment when William, the man that she fell in love with and whom she loved unconditionally, became a living, breathing monster.

She didn't have any answers. It was one in the morning when Megan made up her mind that she would do any and everything in her power to save William from his demons. She would show him how much she loved him by standing by him. After all, that is what marriage is all about right? For better or for worse; in sickness and in health. Right now William was sick and this was their 'worse'.

It was up to her to be strong and hold her marriage together. God would be so pleased with her, she was doing the right thing, she was doing the honorable thing, and was doing exactly what God expected her to do.

Michelle was so excited that she could hardly sleep. Finally, finally Megan would be away from William and start to get her life back on track. Michelle was even excited about helping Megan find a good divorce lawyer. Counseling, lots of counseling and then Megan would well be on her way to finding a man, a good man, not a drunk, not a woman beating, baby killing man like William.

Michelle could hardly contain her excitement; Megan was going to have a great new life, the life that she deserved. Filled with happiness, peace, and lots of love and romance. Michelle drifted off to sleep, and didn't realize that she had been asleep the entire night until the phone startled her awake.

"This better be good, for God's sake it is the middle of the night!" Michelle exclaimed.
"Michelle, it is eight in the morning, what are you babbling about?"
"Oh it is you Megan; did you say 8 o'clock?"
"Yes, I said eight; now wake up and talk to me sleepyhead!"

Michelle slowly sat up and rubbed her eyes; it was in fact light outside. Megan sounded happy, strangely happy.

"Megan, are you alright? What time do you want me to pick you up? I am going to get the U-Haul truck and dad and I are going to start moving your things, just give me a few minutes to wake up".

"Michelle, that is what I wanted to talk to you about, I am going home to William".

"What the fuck did you just say?"

"C'mon Michelle, you don't understand, William is my husband, good or bad he still is. What type of wife would I be if I gave up on him when he needed me the most?"

"But Megan..." Michelle was fully awake now. "Megan, are you for real? What the hell did they give you in that place, better yet, what the hell are you smoking?"

Michelle didn't realize that she was now yelling, so loudly in fact that her mother came knocking on her bedroom door.

"Michelle, what is going on? Can I come in?"
"Yes, come on in, can you believe this shit, excuse my mouth mom, but Megan is actually talking about going back to William!"

"Oh my God no, no, no..." was all Mrs. Hullander could bring herself to say. She broke down in tears.

"See what you did, now mom is hysterical; Megan, don't you do anything until we come to get you, do you hear me? Do not do anything; we are on our way."

CHAPTER 11

Can A Leopard Really Change His Spots?

William walked into the AA meeting for the first time in his life. The pain that he was feeling was unbearable. How did he allow it to come to this? When was the exact hour, minute, second? When was the exact moment that he became his father?

He sat in the circle; they were about to begin, but all William could think about was going home and finishing that bottle of vodka sitting on the kitchen counter. He wanted it so bad that he started to sweat.

He became self conscious and fidgety, but no one was staring, no one seem to think anything was wrong. It took a while for him to come to the realization that *everyone* here was going through the same thing; so of course he looked normal.

"Hi, my name is Brent.......and I am an alcoholic"

"Hi, my name is Donald, and I am an alcoholic"

"Hey everyone, I am Sandra and I am an alcoholic, drunk, whatever you want to call me, I just love the hell out of a good drink."

"What's up? I am Paul and I am a alcoholic; but why do I have to give my name if this is Alcoholics *Anonymous*?" At that quip from Paul, a young man who looked to be barely out of his teen years, everyone laughed and some of the tension and embarrassment in the room was eased a bit.

He added, with what sounded like some type of Caribbean accent,

"Where I come from, we drink from sun up to sun down and aint nabody na blasted alcoholics, we just call we self drunks; aint na meetings nor nothing so. I use to go to de shop, I was na more than 6 or 7, and buy rum fa me father and he friends, and when I get back wid de bottle,, dey use to mek me tek de first shot and……"

This pleasant looking middle aged woman quickly interrupted Paul, "Hello, my name is Hattie and I am an alcoholic, 15 years sober. Paul you will have a chance to tell us everything later, right now we are just introducing ourselves….ok?"

"Ok, na problem, nice to meet everyone" Paul said defeatedly.

William cleared his throat and opened his mouth, but no words came out.

"It's ok man, we aint going to judge you" Paul calmly said. "We all in da same boat here paddling like crazy."

"I am…..I mean, my name is William and…..and….and…this is bullshit, I am in control of my life, I don't need a group of people to tell me what the fuck I need to do!"

He got up and walked out the door. Within 15 minutes of walking through his door, that bottle of vodka was almost gone. This time was different though, William was crying his eyes out. He was suddenly this hurt little boy with no one to turn to; someone whom no one understood, and worse yet, who everybody hated.

That was William's first real attempt at Alcoholics Anonymous.

CHAPTER 12

REDEMPTION SONG

When Megan got out of the cab, she was visibly weak and very fragile. But she calmly walked up to her front door and walked in. William was sitting on the couch with his head buried in his hands crying. Megan immediately ran over to him and held him like he was a lost child.

"Megan, I am so sorry, if you leave me forever I deserve it; I treated you like a dog, I caused you to lose our precious babies, I caused you so much pain that I do not deserve to live".

"Oh William, hush, hush, for better or for worse, remember? I am not going to quit on this marriage, I am not going to quit on you. I am here for you William, these are tests we are going through; God wants the family to be together and he wants me to do everything in my power to make my marriage work."

"Please forgive me Megan, forgive me please; I will spend the rest of my life proving to you how sorry I am. How did we get to this point of so much pain? Help me Megan, please help me, this alcohol is killing me, I cannot stop".

"William, we have to try really hard, we have to fight this one day at a time; we have to overcome this demon; please William, we can do this together". Megan was now sobbing out loud.

They held onto each other and rocked back and forth for what seemed like an eternity.

The rest of the year was somewhat of a challenge for everyone. Megan had done everything but completely put aside her entire family. The elder Mr. Hullander wasn't taking it so well; to the point of on more than one occasion he thought he was having a heart attack.

Worrying day in and day out took a toll on both him and his wife. They looked like they had both aged ten years.

Michelle was the only one who saw Megan anymore. And she had to completely go out of her way to connect with her. She still couldn't wrap her mind around the fact that Megan had actually given up everything and everyone and stayed with William. What the hell is she thinking? Is she living in fear? Is she brainwashed? Is she under the influence of something?

Try as she might, Michelle couldn't find one single reason to justify Megan's reasons for staying with her sorry excuse for a husband.

Michelle even sought counseling herself to try to get a better understanding of why Megan was doing what she was doing. She still didn't have any answers.

William had been clean for almost a year. It was the hardest thing he had ever done in his life. In fact, he and Megan had joined a church and were trying to work their way back to a healthy marriage.

He still couldn't understand why Megan had given him this chance after all he had put her through. She had even become estranged from her own family for him. Michelle backed off and had told her parents to do the same. They all felt helpless and somewhat hopeless, but they had to leave Megan and William alone.

William and Megan had come such a long way, that they started to look into adoption. They talked about it briefly, but knew that because of their troubled life that no agency would ever consider placing a child with them. Even though Megan was working hard on making her marriage work, she could forgive but she couldn't bring herself to forget.

When William was asleep next to her, she would stare at him with such hatred burning in her soul that she was ashamed of herself. She kept asking herself why she chose to go through this so-called reconciliation, why was she pretending to be the perfect little forgiving wife, why was she giving up everything for this man who had all but taken everything away from her.

On nights like these, when sleep was a long way away, and her brain refused to shut off, Megan would go into the bathroom and lock the door. She would then, sit on the floor with her knees pulled up to her chin and rock back and forth.

She would occasionally hold her belly, the belly that would never carry another child, the belly that would never feel a mother's love, the belly that held pain, sorrow, regret, hatred, forgiveness and so much sadness that it was becoming unbearable.

Megan was getting to a point where through counseling, much, much prayer and self realization that she wanted to start living for Megan. Not what her parents or sister or brother expected, not what William expected, not even what her counselor expected, but what she wanted. But what did she want?

Deep down inside she knew that it was just a matter of time before William became William once again. But why was she waiting? Was Michelle right? Was William going to eventually kill her? Do they really have a "happily ever after" written in the stars somewhere?

These were too many questions that Megan wanted answered; so she just gave up and decided to live one day at a time, all the while secretly hoping and praying that William would just simply drop dead.

CHAPTER 13

Michelle's Turn

Mr. Hullander was having major health problems, but he somehow managed to keep it mostly to himself. After Megan reconciled with William, Mr. Hullander started losing sleep, losing more of his hair and was constantly having chest pains. Michelle and her mother became increasingly worried about him, but he always managed to reassure them that he was fine and just having a bit of indigestion.

Michelle in the meantime was busy with her own life. She started dating a wonderful man, Brent, whom she had met through a mutual friend, and she was getting out a lot more. Yes, she was worried about her father and her sister, but she finally faced the fact that it had all but consumed her. She couldn't continue to jump each time the phone rang, in fear that it might be "that call" about Megan; or wondering if her father was going to have a stroke.

Michelle had to start living without the dark cloud hanging over her head. Once her mind was made up to do that, she became more relaxed and accepted Brent's invitation for dinner.

She was not expecting much, but after a few weeks of long talks, long walks and sharing their hopes and dreams, they realize that they were both falling hard. Brent, a Pharmacist, came from a stable family, with no drama whatsoever. Michelle remembered the good old days when her own family was drama free.

An only child, he couldn't even begin to understand the dynamics of Michelle's relationship with her sister. He knew enough to know that it was something he could not relate to but he developed an understanding through Michelle.

When Michelle felt comfortable enough to discuss Megan's troubled life, he was appalled and a bit disgusted that a man, any man, could possibly treat a woman the way Michelle claimed that Megan's husband treated her.

But he decided to just listen intently, but offer no solid opinions. He was a man who knew when to keep his mouth shut. He was starting to fall in love with Michelle; deep down inside he wanted nothing more than to marry her and take her away from all this stress and family drama.

Brent was planning his future with Michelle. She didn't know it but he had already met privately with her parents to ask for her hand in marriage.

"Forgive me if I am not too thrilled Brent, but our other daughter isn't exactly the poster child for marriage; so if I am not excited don't be too hard on me" said a tired, worn out looking Mr. Hullander.

"Honey, don't be so negative; Brent, my main concern is that you have only been seeing Michelle for a few months now, and you suddenly want to marry her?" chimed in Mrs. Hullander.

"Mam, when you meet someone and you start dating and there is an instant connection, why wait a year, or two years? Is there a specific time frame to date to ensure that a marriage will work?"

"That is not what we are saying Brent, we are simply questioning your true feelings for Michelle".

"I have only known Michelle for a mere five months, but from the first time I placed my eyes on her, I knew that she was the one. It was just a matter of time, and I was right. Now I cannot picture moving forward without her in my life."

Mr. Hullander sighed, "Brent, I give you my blessing, because I do not think that you could be any worse, than Megan's husband".

"Amen to that" said Mrs. Hullander.

"With all due respect, I would appreciate it if you never ever compare me to that man again; I have never met him, but from what I do know, he seem to be the devil himself. So do not EVER compare me to him again."

With that, Mr. and Mrs. Hullander looked at each other; each relieved that Michelle was about to have a caring, loving husband; but with it came a sad reminder of Megan's situation.

"I don't know if I can survive in your family", Brent and Michelle were out having dinner and Michelle was inadvertently blabbing on and on about Megan and her problems. Brent had had enough; sure he loved Michelle, but he was starting to wonder what their life was going to be like with Megan always in the shadows, and Michelle always worrying and stressed out about her sister.

"Brent, how could you say that?"

"Let's face it and be honest about it, Michelle you are consumed by your sister's life!"

"What do you expect me to do? Am I supposed to just let him kill her?"

"That's not what I am saying Michelle, I am just saying that I am right here in front of you and we have a lot of planning to do and a lot to talk about, but you insist on lamenting over Megan's life, a life that SHE chose".

"I don't expect you to understand, you are an only child; Megan is my sister and I want her safe", Michelle was now in tears.

"Michelle, everyone wants her to be safe, but what everyone is forgetting is that Megan has to first want to be safe. Megan made her choice and like it or not everyone has to respect and accept that".

"Accept? Accept? Brent if I saw you walking into the path of a bus I would push you from in front of it….."

Brent cut her off, "chances are if I am walking in front of a bus I have no idea that the bus is coming; on the other hand, Megan knows EXACTLY what she is in".

"...but, but"

"No buts here, Megan is a grown ass woman, and if she chooses to live that kind of life, and is well aware of the consequences then just leave her the hell alone".

Sensing Michelle's hurt, he added in a much calmer tone,

"Just let her live her life how she sees fit, be it wrong or right in someone else's eyes. Michelle she is an adult, and even though I understand and respect your love and concern I think that if you do not let go, this is going to end up hurting you more that it hurts her".

"I am tired Brent, take me home" was all Michelle said.

CHAPTER 14

A Little Too Late

Megan had perfected her plan a long time ago. Actually deep down, her mind was made up the day she checked out of the Psychiatric hospital. She was leaving William.

She had heard somewhere that when your hand is in the lion's mouth that you slowly ease it out inch by inch; you never just yank it out.

For the past eight months she was making preparations to get away from her husband, and she was easing out inch by inch. She kept it from her family; deciding once and for all that she had endured enough and was a fool for way too long.

Megan had also come to the realization that she was not and could not be William's savior. She needed saving first and by God she was going to save herself.

Megan's decision was derived from everything everyone around her had been telling her for so many years, and the fact that she could run from the truth for only so long.

For months she had been hauling her belongings, sometimes one or two pieces at a time, to a storage unit. She couldn't just pack and leave; it had to be done so that William didn't have a clue.

William was really trying to be a good husband, and Megan started to feel that tug and pull on her heart strings, but only briefly. She didn't know what came over her, but somehow she was able to harden her heart towards him. She had stopped talking to her family, mainly because William had convinced her that they were meddling in the marriage and giving her wrong advice. But now she was not talking to them because she was protecting them.

After months of fake laughs, fake sex, fake everything, Megan was finally ready to make her escape, and William did not have a clue. She had decided to go to Camille's house. William would never look for her there. He knew that they were not speaking, or so he thought.

Megan had apologized to Camille over and over again, and Camille was more than happy to have her best friend back in her life. Other than Megan's psychiatrist, Camille was the only one who knew of her getaway plans.

They had to be careful not to be seen together, they did not want William to get the faintest idea what was going on.

Finally, after almost a year of planning and procrastinating and more planning and even more procrastinating, Megan was finally ready to make her move. Her plans were in motion. She would first move in with Camille across town, then immediately file a restraining order against William. She was then going to buy a gun. Buying the gun was an afterthought.

On a warm summer morning, Megan waited patiently for William to leave for work. Camille was waiting around the corner. Megan did not take all her belongings. Her keepsakes and larger items were in storage and she had one suitcase and one bag with her.

When she saw Camille pull up outside, she placed the key under the mat and rushed out the door and into the car.

"Have you told Michelle yet?"

"No, I do not want to get her involved. If William thinks for a second that my family helped me, they could be in danger".

"I know Megan, but they do deserve to know that you are ok. I can call Michelle for you if you want".

By now Megan was in tears.

"Please do, and tell her that I will call her really soon".

"And Camille?"

"Yes?"

"Tell her that I love her very much".

CHAPTER 15

Why?

The doorbell rang, Mr. Hullander got up and slowly made his way to answer it. He figured it was the mailman just needing a signature. He was not prepared to find William on his doorstep.

"What do you want?"

"My wife, is she here?"

"No". Mr. Hullander attempted to close the door, but William stuck his foot inside the door.

By this time Michelle had made her way downstairs after hearing the loud voices.

"What's going on?"

"You are hiding her, I know it".

"Megan is not here William, please leave".

"I am not leaving without my wife, you all have brainwashed her".

William tried to push his way past Michelle and her father, but Michelle managed to stop him. By now she was fuming, but scared. What William didn't know was that even though Megan was not staying there, that she had stopped by for a brief visit.

Mr. Hullender shouted to Michelle to call the police and to grab his shotgun. Megan was listening to everything from the top of the stairs. She could not put her family in danger. It was her that he wanted, and if going with him meant her family would be safe, then she had no choice.

Michelle was yelling at the top of her lungs and William who was clearly under the influence of something was directly in her face. Mr. Hullender was trying to make his way to get his shotgun.

Megan suddenly appeared,

"William, please leave my family alone. It is me you want".

"Tell your bitch sister to get out of my way".

"William please, if you leave I promise I will come home"

"No, you are coming with me, now".

"She is not going anywhere with you", Michelle yelled.

Megan saw it first. The evil in William's eyes, she had experienced it many times before.

Oh my God, he is going to hit Michelle!

Megan started down the stairs, just as William grabbed Michelle by the throat and slammed her head against the wall. The sound of Michelle's skull making contact with the corner of the wall was sickening. Michelle slumped to the floor, motionless.

"Oh my God, Michelle, Michelle please answer me", Megan was hysterical.

Mr. Hullender heard the screaming and hurried as fast as he could, only to find his daughter on the floor, blood slowly oozing from her head. Megan was cradling Michelle in her arms and screaming at the top of her lungs for William to leave.

When she looked up at him again, all she saw was what appeared to be a gun. Darkness.

WHERE AM I?

Megan looked up; Michelle was no longer in her arms. Michelle was now walking towards her. Megan screamed. She just knew that she was dreaming.

"Megan, I think we are…."

"No, no".

"Who are these other women?"

"Oh Michelle we are not dead, are we? I am so sorry, this is all my fault".

"Megan, nothing happens that is not meant to happen".

"Why Michelle, why?"

By now the other ladies were all looking on, shocked..

"Megan, everything happens for a reason, but it is not your time. God has given you many, many chances because you have a purpose in life. This is still not your time Megan."

"No Michelle, I want to stay with you."

"You have a lot of living to do Megan, trust me. You suffered long enough, it is now your turn at happiness. Tell mom and dad that I was honored to have them as my parents and they were the best."

Michelle hugged her sister.

By now Megan was in a daze; if she thought that this was strange, one of the women, the one named Sheldon walked up and spoke to her.

"Megan, please take care of my children for me. Be there for everything that I will miss; and remind them everyday that I love them. Tell them that my love never died."

"What…what are you talking about? This is a bad dream and I want to wake up".

Once again Megan woke up in the hospital surrounded by her parents, her brother and Camille. But no Michelle.

NEXT: Meet Alex and Brea. The story continues…